THE
AWAKENING
DRAGON KNIGHT CHRONICLES
——◆•◆—— BOOK 1 ——◆•◆——

ANDREW WICHLAND

Andrew Wichland

THE
AWAKENING
DRAGON KNIGHT CHRONICLES
—•◦•——— BOOK 1 ———•◦•—

FRAIL HOPE

EIRIAN FLEW THROUGH the night as fast as her large wings would allow. As often as she could, she looked over her shoulder. In the moonlight behind her horned tail, she saw two figures flying after her. Even though they were still miles away, they were slowly catching up.

She turned her head back around, placed one of paws against her lower abdomen, and thought about her unborn children. Her wings were beginning to strain. As she flew above a sea of trees, a sharp pain ranked through her lower abdomen.

"No, not now, it's too early; just a little longer, my children," she pleaded of them. However, the pain increased, and she faltered a little in her flight and ducked behind a hill.

Relieved to spot her destination, she began her descent to a clearing. She landed awkwardly on three paws, because the fourth paw clutched a box. Folding her wings, she surveyed the area. Trees of monstrous size surrounded her. A stone gateway was set about forty feet behind a smooth crystal, which was nearly ten feet in diameter. Along the edge of the crystal, lines of runes ran along the side. At the top, sides and the bottom four lines of runes crossed to meet at a circle in the middle.

Eirian quickly hopped forward to the crystal, arched her neck, and brought her head down. When she opened her mouth, fire shot from it, enveloping the crystal. Then she closed her mouth, stopped the bombardment of fire, and hopped back. Now the runes were shining like the moon. Five beams of light shot from the crystal to the stone gateway and ran along the inner frame. After a moment, the beams met at the center, and the gateway formed a light that flowed like water.

"We're almost out, my children; just a little longer," she said.

A fresh wave of pain ran through her body, and as fast as she could, she hopped forward on three legs and passed through the gateway. She emerged on a small mountainside on a different planet.

For the rest of the known Galaxy the planet she was now on was known as Ta Jar. But like all planets that housed a non-magical settlement it now had a different name. To all free people it was known as Amal.

Once again, trees filled the area, but she saw a small town in front of her. It appeared to be less than a mile away.

She collapsed onto her side and hummed a tune as her body began to change. Her forelegs and paws turned into arms and hands, while her hind legs and paws became legs and feet. Her spikes shrank into her body, and her horns disappeared into her skull, where light-brown hair flowed out. Her tail pulled into her spine, while her snout shrank and formed into a nose. Her scales turned into white skin, and her wings surrounded her and became a light-blue, flowing robe.

All the while, her body had shrunk in size until she was almost five times shorter in length and almost twelve times thinner than her true body. However, two things remained the same. Her swollen belly and her eyes were still as violet as her scales had been.

When the transformation was complete, Eirian stood up on her bare feet and looked down at the village. Holding onto her belly, and still clutching the gold-embroidered, wooden box, she started her descent.

How can humans stand just having two legs? she thought, as she stumbled through the streets of the village. The moon was still out, and some of the villagers stared at her as she walked through the night.

Ignoring their looks, she quickly got out of the streets as hover cars went by. She stopped at a small, single-story, shingle-roofed house. The front of the house stood on stilts, and a small flight of steps led up to the porch. She stumbled up the steps and banged on the door. After several long moments, a light turned on inside, and a shadow moved under the door.

The door finally opened, revealing a woman who was struggling to pull on her bathrobe. She appeared to be of Asian descent, and Eirian guessed that she was in her late twenties or early thirties. She wore a kind smile despite the fact that she had clearly been awoken in the middle of the night.

"May I help you?" the woman asked as she tied the sash.

Seconds later, a man joined her at the door. He wore a pair of pajama pants, but his broad, muscular chest and arms were bare. He was also of Asian descent and was a head taller than the woman at his side.

"Chikako, who is it? It's almost one," said the man, but he stopped when he saw Eirian and his eyes went wide. "Eirian?" he muttered. The woman at his side looked at him.

"Jun, my old friend, I need your help," Eirian said. Then she fell, and Jun caught her before she hit the ground as another contraction went through her body.

The man brought her inside the house. He led her into the bedroom and helped her get settled on a sleeping mat.

"Who is this woman, Jun?" Chikako said.

"She's an old friend, Chikako. Now go wake the doctor. She's in labor," Jun said.

Eirian reached out and grabbed his arm tightly. "No . . .

doctor . . . you . . . must . . . do . . . it . . ." she said through gritted teeth. Then she threw her head back in pain.

Jun looked at Eirian for a moment as she writhed on his bed. Then he turned to Chikako.

"Honey, get me a bowl of water, some string, scissors, clean washcloths, and soft blankets. Hurry!"

Chikako quickly left the room, and he turned back to Eirian. She gripped his hand tightly, and he said, "It'll be alright," but as she was engulfed by another wave of pain, she wasn't sure if his words were intended to reassure her or himself.

Almost four hours later, Eirian was drenched in sweat, and the lower part of her robe was soaked in both sweat and blood. Weakly, she leaned back on her elbows and then slowly reached out for her two sons and her daughter, whom Chikako had wrapped in soft blankets. As she held them in her arms, tears ran down her face. She took a deep breath and then looked from her three children to her friend Jun and his wife, Chikako.

"They're beautiful, aren't they?" she asked them as she gazed at the babies.

"Just like their mother," Jun said, and Chikako nodded, smiling broadly.

"Jun, there is a particular reason I came to you and your wife," Eirian said. She tried to hide the desperation in her voice. "I must ask you something."

"What?" Jun asked. His expression showed that he dreaded what she was going to say.

Trying to smile, she laid down her youngest two children and held out her first-born. "Raise my first-born as you would your own."

Before he could reply, she added, "My other son and daughter must be separated, too. Give my second- and third-born to trusted families in another village, and give those friends the same instructions I will give you now. Don't tell any of the children that they're one of three until they're ready to know."

She reached beside her for the wooden box and opened it. Inside were eight bracelets, each with a different colored crystal in the center. The sides of each bracelet had a different design and little raised engravings of weapons.

She showed her friends the bracelets. "You'll know when the time is right when they receive their bracelets. Make sure they grow big and strong, and don't tell them about me until they're ready," she said. Then she broke into sobs.

Chikako and Jun reached out and took the children from her. Immediately, she covered her mouth and started humming a tune. When she drew her hand away, she held three teeth in her palm. Unlike human teeth, these were an inch long, curved back, and sharp: dragon teeth.

"Along with other things, these will protect them and help them find each other," she said.

Holding the dragon teeth as if they were made of glass, she slipped one into each of the children's blankets. Gingerly, Eirian climbed to her feet, took a few wobbling steps forward, and looked down at her two sons and daughter. Tears overflowed down her face as she bent down and kissed her children.

She then looked up at the couple. "Thank you for doing this for me. Five others will be chosen besides my sons and daughter. I must go now." She headed for the door.

"Eirian, you just gave birth. You should rest," Chikako said, stepping forward to stop her.

As Eirian reached the door, she stopped, but she didn't even look back. "If they find me here, it won't take them long to find my children. I must go in order to protect my children and the village from them. I pray I'll see the children again." Then she left the house.

At first, she walked down the street, but soon she was running, tears flowing like a river down her cheeks. When she reached a safe distance from the village, she began to sing the same song that she'd hummed after entering the planet. A few moments later, she spread her wings, once more a dragon, and flew back to the gateway.

As she approached the area, she took a deep breath and released a ball of fire at the crystal, which opened the gateway. She flew through the gateway and back where she'd come from, back into the night sky. As she soared over the trees, she spotted her pursuers coming her way.

Now it's time to fight, she thought. Anger replaced her sense of loss at giving up her children, and she sped toward them.

Just before the two dragons reached her, they broke formation, one heading left, the other right. In response, she banked to the side. Swinging her tail forward, she nailed one dragon in the head with her horned tail. As he fell to the ground, his head caved in, and she turned sharply and fell in behind the other dragon.

The two weaved all over the sky as the remaining dragon tried to get her off his tail. When she got close enough, she arched her neck a little, took a deep breath, and aimed her head forward, fire racing from her mouth. Before the fire reached him, however, he peeled and shot up. Then he twisted back down, connecting hard with her back and buckling her wings.

As they plummeted to the earth, the battle continued. She tried to get her jaws around his neck, and he aimed for hers.

"Don't mess with this mom!" Eirian growled. Using her wings, she forced her opponent to the ground and kicked off with her hind legs.

His back hit the ground first, knocking down a few trees with a series of loud crashes and a single loud crack.

Muscles straining, she spread her wings with a snap like thunder. She sailed forward a little before crashing hard onto the ground. Her wings brushed against the trees, and dirt and debris flew everyone. When the dust, branches, and leaves finally settled, she gingerly climbed to her paws. She tested her wings and flinched in pain.

At least my sons and daughter are safe from the Black Dragon, she thought. *Still, he won't be happy when he learns his two goons failed to capture me. And if he finds out I gave birth, he'll start looking for all of them, not just me.*

She folded her wings and galloped away as fast as she could.

In the house on stilts, Chikako comforted the fitful baby in her arms. "What should we call him? Eirian didn't name him."

Jun reached for the baby. As he held his new adopted son, the baby opened his eyes.

"I name you Alac—Alac-Ryuu," he said, and Alac cooed.

Chikako picked up the other newborns. She said, "Jun, they're all lovely children. Do

we really have to separate them?"

Jun looked at her and nodded. "Yes, unfortunately, we do. I'll send the younger boy to a friend of mine, and the girl will go to a friend of yours. If they stay together, the Black Dragon will find them quickly."

"Who was that woman? And what makes these children so important?" Chikako pulled up a chair and sat across from Jun at their table.

"I can't explain it now, but trust me, they're important. In fact, they're more important than either of us can possibly imagine," he said.

He rose from the table and carefully placed each child gently on the mat. Then he returned to the table, took the box, and opened the lid.

Chikako peered inside. "What are they, anyway?"

Jun closed the box carefully. "The keys to their future."

CHAPTER 1
ALAC-RYUU JUN YAMAMOTO

Twelve years, three hundred sixty-four days later

THE SUN ROSE over the house on stilts. Inside the house were signs of happiness. On the mantel piece over the fire-place, a brigade of photos showed bits and pieces of this family's life together: a little boy in a hover stroller posing with his parents, taking his first step, playing with his father, dancing on his mother's shoes.

The sun's light crept into one of the rooms and fell onto the closed eyes of a twelve-year-old boy. When he was in school, his teachers and family called him Alac or Alac-Ryuu, but to his closest friends he was just Ryuu or Robin. He turned over on his mat, try-ing to get more sleep, and then heard a knock on his door.

"Alac! Time to get up, honey! Breakfast is almost ready."

It was his mother. Alac groaned and pulled the blankets over his head.

"Alac-Ryuu Jun Yamamoto, get your butt out of bed now and come to breakfast!" Her voice was kind despite the command. Then he heard her walk away.

He smiled and climbed out of bed. As he gazed briefly in the small bedroom mirror, he saw that the curved tooth, which was hanging from a necklace, shined white on his well-toned chest. His body was muscular from years of training and hard labor. A short while later he climbed out of the shower wrapping a towel around his waist. Hair wet from the water.

After wiping some steam from the mirror to brush his teeth. His eyes drifted down to the counter. Where his light dampening contacts and white noise plugs were.

For a second he looked he eyed them. Before shaking his head and leaving the bathroom. Back in his room, he grabbed some clothes from the closet and started to get dressed.

Walking down the hall, he stopped in front of a larger mirror to adjust his dark hair, which went down to his shoulders. He pulled out a strip of leather and tied his hair back. His face had a savage type of beauty. His features were sharp and angled, particularly around his eyes and ears, which were slightly pointed at the top, middle, and bottom, giving them a backwards stroking angle. Sometimes when he looked in the mirror, the intenseness of his features startled him, but the thing he liked most about his appearance was his hazel eyes. They were a mix of different colors that seemed to shift at random. He looked in the mirror often to see what colors he could get out of them.

Nevertheless, he didn't place all of his focus on his good looks. In school, he had already jumped twelve grades ahead. Now he attended his father's school, which was hidden high in the mountains. He did pretty well in his classes, but sometimes the others made fun of him for his age, for being the head teacher's son, and for the unusual shape of his ears.

As he finished tying his hair back, he paused and lowered his gaze, thinking back to when he had first started at the academy. He had been only five, but even then he was as tall as a teenager and six times stronger than a man. As much as his rapid development had scared most of the village, it had frightened him more.

He remembered walking into the academy as a new student. The older students constantly stared at him, though some showed more curiosity than derision. Now, eight years later, at the verge of thirteen, he already had the body of an eighteen-year-old but had only gotten stronger and a diamond-sharp mind. Still, instead of gaining more acceptance at the school, in some ways things just got worse.

Shrugging off the memory, he continued down the hall, pulling on his jacket. When he entered the kitchen, his mother was serving pancakes to his dad. Jun was now in his late thirties. Like Ryuu, he was muscular in body, although Ryuu knew he had far to go before he would ever catch up to his father's experience.

His mother had long hair, which she also tied back in a ponytail. She was beautiful, with a slim body. Ryuu knew, however, that her willowy appearance was misleading, because it distracted observers from her broad shoulders and the rolling muscles under her olive skin. In truth, she was just as strong as her husband. She also served as one of Ryuu's teachers, although she preferred to work with him at home, avoiding any possible encounters with the drifters, smugglers, and pirates who frequently landed on their planet to give and take food and supplies.

"Morning, Dad," Ryuu said, sitting at the table opposite his father.

"Morning, Alac. It's good to see you out of bed."

His mother put the plate of pancakes on the table. Ryuu served himself a few and reached for the maple syrup. Then he looked up at his parents and grinned.

"Soooo, you guys doing anything later?" Ryuu asked them.

His father shook his head. "Apart from your exam tonight—which you should be getting ready for—nothing much." He turned his attention back to his pancakes.

"What about tomorrow?" Ryuu asked. He picked up his fork and took a bite.

His mother said, "Well, I promised the neighbor I would help her redesign her kitchen tomorrow. I'll be out all day."

His father tapped his fork against the table. Then he smacked his hand to his forehead. "Wait—tomorrow is a special day!" he said.

His mother stared at them, a look of shock on her face slowly appearing.

Ryuu smiled. *It's about time,* he thought.

Then his mother snapped her fingers and pointed at Jun. "Yeah, it someone's birthday tomorrow, isn't it? I hope she doesn't think we've forgotten!" She took a bite of her pancakes.

"Ah, that's . . . err . . . *she?*" Ryuu said, smile fading.

His father nodded. "It's an instructor's birthday is tomorrow." He turned to Chikako. "Don't worry; I bought her a fruit basket. Remind me to give it to her."

Ryuu looked down at his food, disappointed. *They forgot.*

Soon after, Ryuu grabbed his sky surfer. Based on vintage photos from history books, he had concluded that, when open, it looked like an old-fashioned surfboard without the rudder, but in its collapsed position, it looked like a small, box-shaped plate about a foot wide and tall. Most important, it had the ability to fly. It was not as powerful as a sky rider, which was for racing and transport, but it was enough for recreation.

"Don't forget. You need to be ready for the exam by nine this evening," his father called out to him as he raced for the door.

"You got it, Dad!" Ryuu said. He bolted down the stairs, jumping the last few.

"And I want you back here at least two hours before that," his mother called. "Seven p.m. Okay?" She handed him a bag. "I've packed you a lunch. Maybe you and your friends can have a picnic."

"Thanks, Mom." He stuffed it into his backpack. Then he headed down the stairs, and the door swung shut.

He knew he would have to carry the sky surfer until he reached the village gates. Outside his house, he met up with one of his best friends, Bryan. Bryan was almost a head taller than him, with lighter skin that rippled with bulging, toned muscles. He had dark-red hair and brown eyes.

"Hey, Ryuu!" he said, and they grasped hands.

"Hey, LJ!" he said. "Ready to go meet the others?"

"Ryuu, you are *not* Robin Hood, and I am *not* Little John!" Bryan said. He smiled and added, "You read those books way too much. Just because you're the best shot and swordsman in the class and I'm the best staff man doesn't mean we should change our names."

They began to run, dodging a few people on the street. When one shouted after them, Ryuu stopped running and turned to his friend.

"I'm serious, LJ. Books and movies like *Robin Hood* give people hope. They remind them that folks can rise from the ashes of their loss. These heroes have one goal: to help save the oppressed and innocent from those who would do them harm. These are men of honor who have lost everything. But iinstead of seeking revenge, they've devoted themselves to saving the lives that tyrants like the Black Dragon and his Sentinels target."

He shifted his weight and continued. "That's why I read those books; they give me hope for a bright future where we don't have to be afraid—where we don't have to look over our shoulders for an enemy who could be anyone we know."

Ryuu knew that Bryan had suffered more than any of his other friends. His entire family had been slaughtered by the Black Drag-on's Sentinels when their caravan was attacked. Bryan had escaped only because of his parents' courage and faith to launch him out of the last escape pod. Now he lived with one of the many foster families in town.

Like so many refugees calling Amal home.

"You're right, Ryuu," Bryan said. "I understand. And I was just teasing. You can call me LJ whenever you want."

Then he grinned and the mood lightened. "Now come on, *Robin,* we've got to meet the others. Allison says that her brother has upgrades for the sky riders."

They raced each other down the center street, dodging hover cars and bikes as they went, showing off a few of the skills they had learned in school. In synchronized motion, Ryuu and Bryan flipped onto the hood of a hover car, ran along it, leapt forward, rolled along the ground, and continued running. The pair then darted for the sidewalk. People leaped out of their way, with some frowning at them while other emitted bursts of laughter.

Soon they exited the village gates, pressed a button, and threw their sky surfers ahead of them. The units extended automatically, with the front curved and the thrusters behind. The sky surfers hovered in the air as the boys, still running, leapt forward onto them.

As Ryuu landed, with his legs bent and his back heel pressed on the starter, his feet were bound down. Then, as the jets fired, the boys rocketed forward. They cheered as they soared up and above the trees, weaving left and right. They soon came to the stone arch in the woods that stood next to the crystal embedded in the ground.

Standing next to the crystal and leaning against the arch were the rest of their friends, and Ryuu seized this second opportunity to show off. He leaned back on his board and shot higher into the air at a vertical angle at breakneck speed. Then, at the height of his climb, he pressed the button again with his foot, and the engine died.

Ryuu closed his eyes, and a dreamy expression came over his face as he tumbled back to the ground. He twisted, flipped, and spun as he dropped faster and faster from the sky to the ground.

Finally, he grabbed the nose of the board and spun a circle, increasing in speed even more.

At the last second, as he approached the tree line, he slammed his heel onto the button, and the sky surfer dipped below the trees. Ryuu weaved left and right, avoiding the trees and branches as he sped forward through the forest. He broke out of the trees by zooming between two tightly spaced branches and out into the clearing, where he whizzed through the gateway, his friends cheering. He circled the clearing once and then landed with the board hovering about a foot in the air.

His friend Allison was as tall as him. She had short, dark-brown hair, which shifted over her elven ears, and a muscular body which rippled under her ebony skin and grace that almost matched Ryuu's. Her beautiful face, which included dark-blue eyes, usually caught the attention of the boys in school, but most wouldn't dare approach her for a date. In fact, she had broken the finger of the last guy who had done so.

She was one of the top students in school, but her progress was sometimes halted by her temper, which was on a shorter fuse than Ryuu's. In class, she tended to be the first to volunteer answers without thinking, and outside class she was known for barreling into reckless decisions with hardly ever thinking about them.

The two grasped hands. "Ryuu, you're one gutsy guy. I like that; it reminds me of me." They laughed.

"Now I know I'm in trouble," Ryuu said.

Allison's twin brother, Eric, came up and joined them. While Eric had more muscles and the broad chest of a young man, he generally matched his twin's appearance right down to the last hair on his head.

Allison, quick to fight, often stepped up to the plate while Eric puzzled things out from an intellectual point of view. He and Ryuu were top of the class in schoolwork. As well, Eric was a martial arts champion who was second to none with tonfa sticks.

Ryuu looked at the last friend of the group: Aiolos. Known as the class clown, he was still quick-witted and did well in school even though the teachers needed to bring his attention back to the lesson every five minutes or so. Aiolos was a free-spirited blonde, whose carefree approach to life managed to clash enough with Allison's reckless one that sometimes the two friends were at odds. Ryuu always appreciated his friend's good nature, particularly during tough times. Now he and Aiolos grasped hands and pulled into a back-slapping hug.

Aiolos stepped back, looked at Ryuu, and smiled widely. "Ryuu, your success with that nose grab spin was positively inspiring," he said. The others looked at them and nodded.

Ryuu said, "Thanks, man." Then he turned to Eric. "What kind of upgrades do you have for the sky riders?"

Eric smiled at this and walked over to a set of sky riders hovering in the air in a straight line. They looked like various sports motorcycles with no wheels front and back, and each had a small but powerful jet propulsion system where the taillights would have been.

He patted the seat on a bright-yellow one. "Last night I initiated an overwrite of essential system programming. Also, I removed nonessential equipment from the primary source so the velocity should be doubled," Eric said.

Allison looked at Ryuu. "You speak Geek, so please, I beg you: translate for the rest of us."

Then she looked at Eric and added, "No offense, bro."

He shrugged.

Ryuu laughed, shook his head, and tried to explain. "He said that he's stripped them of excess body fat. And he overwrote the thruster protocols, which means that now we can accelerate beyond the original, restricted speeds. In other words, he's given us some sweet rides now."

The group cheered and Eric gave a bow.

They immediately decided to test out the modifications that Eric had made. However, before Ryuu put his helmet on, he grabbed Eric by the elbow and said, "You did put them at a speed where the thrusters won't have a meltdown, right? The thrusters were set at those speeds by the manufacturer for that very reason. So you didn't exceed that heat buildup, did you?"

Eric smiled. "Why do you think I removed that extra weight?" Then he placed a half ring around his neck and pressed a button on the side.

Blue-colored metal plates with flames began to slide up and along the sides of his head, but they left a gap around the top half of his face. When the plates reached the ring around his neck and connected, an inflating sound occurred, and padding expanded from the inside. On the side of the head, a panel slid back, revealing three buttons one on top of the other.

Eric pressed the middle one, a black-shaded visor lowered into place, and he hopped onto the blue bike.

Ryuu sighed as he climbed onto his red bike and activated his own helmet, which was red with a gold dragon design. *One of the main ways people can tell they're related, but that's half-elves for you,* he thought.

He pressed the ignition button, and the engine roared to life. Ryuu closed his eyes and smiled at the powerful noise of the engine. He twisted the gas. The engine roared louder, and his smile got wider with the sound of it.

"Ryuu!" It was Allison's voice. He opened his eyes, and there on his visor was a 3-D image of her face.

She gave him a sly smile. "Hey, first one around the mountain is the winner, eh?"

He smiled back. "You got it, Ace. Let's race. The rest of you guys in?" he asked, and images of his other friends popped up on his visor.

"You know it."

"Affirmative."

"You'd have to beat me away with a stick."

"Okay," he said. "One, two, three, GO!" Then he gunned the engine and took off like a flash.

He sped above the forest. After a few seconds, he looked behind him and saw them catching up on their sky riders, with Allison on green, Bryan on yellow, Aiolos on white, and Eric on blue. Soon they were neck and neck, and as they sped on their way, the ground turned into a multicolored blur of endless motion. Ryuu gunned the engine and shot forward. He had no doubt that his friends were still in close pursuit.

Ryuu rolled to the right and went into a light dive when they reached a ravine on the side of the mountain. Alongside his friends, he sped down the ravine at a breakneck pace, dodging the rocks that jetted out at odd angles and formation. They became neck and neck again after Ryuu put his sky rider into a spin and flew through a tight rock hole.

For the next several moments they raced down the ravine in a tight formation, with each one fighting for the lead. Finally, as Ryuu ducked under a rock formation that stretched from both sides, the end of the ravine came into view. They raced on, gunning their engines. The rock wall got closer and they began to run out of space.

At the last second, with Allison in the lead and Ryuu in a close second, they were up and out of the ravine. A few mountain goats being herded by some the villagers were spooked as the friends roared overhead, and the villagers shouted after them. Ryuu laughed with joy as they rocketed into the trees, out of sight from the villagers on the ground.

Now they weaved left and right as they zoomed through the maze of towering mountain trees. Moments later, they burst from the tree line and zoomed upward.

Ryuu lowered his head, then looked ahead again. The group rounded the corner, and once again, they were all neck and neck.

Soon the gateway was in sight. He leaned forward and floored it, shooting forward.

Seconds later, Ryuu and Allison were fighting for supremacy. He was in the lead; she was in the lead. At the last second Ryuu banked up, rolled around Allison, pulled ahead of her, and shot between the two stones a second before her. He thrust his fist into the air, cheering his victory.

He came to a skidding stop and hovered in midair as the rest of the group ground to a halt behind him. Then they formed a circle, facing each other. Ryuu pressed the middle button, and his visor shot up into the helmet. Grinning, he looked at everyone.

"It's okay! You can say it!" He leaned on his bike.

They each raised their visor. Allison rolled her eyes and said, "There goes his ego!" Then she smiled.

Aiolos removed his helmet and grinned.

"Yeah, his helmet is readjusting to fit his newly inflated head!" The sneering voice came over their coms.

Before Ryuu could respond, he heard the rumble of sky riders coming up from the village toward them. He recognized their bikes and turned quickly to his friends.

"Here comes trouble."

CHAPTER 2
TEAM LOCKSLEY

THE RIDERS SPED toward Ryuu's group, halted their bikes, and faced them. The teenager on the rider in front of Ryuu quickly pushed the button of his helmet, which retracted to reveal the short blond hair and handsome face of one of the most popular students in his father's school: Dulgald. One by one, Dulgald's friends followed suit. Most of them were big, strong muscular boys who, despite their bulging muscles, were stupid. The last person in line, facing Allison, was the only girl. She had long blonde hair.

By name, they were Babieca, Bamber, Kade, and Melinda, and none of their smiles looked genuine.

The two groups stared at each other for a few minutes. Finally, Dulgald leaned on his bike and broke the silence.

"So. I see you and your friends still being inflated showoffs, eh, Alac?"

Ryuu smiled. "It's not our fault that you and your friends can't fly, Dulgald. Besides, it's not being a showoff if you can bring it."

Aiolos, who was next to Allison on Ryuu's left, nodded.

At this, Dulgald's expression turned to fury, and he sat up

straight. "We can take you any time. Just name the time," he declared. His friends nodded.

Smiling, Ryuu looked at his friends. He knew that they got his idea when they each nodded, replaced their helmet, and zoomed away.

Dulgald and his friends were clearly curious. In fact, the larger boys looked dumbfounded as they watched Ryuu's friends go.

Ryuu leaned more onto his rider. "They'll be back in twenty minutes. How about when they get back, we play sky hockey, you against us. First team to reach ten wins."

Dulgald grinned. "Fine, you're on. See you in twenty." Then he pressed the button on his helmet ring, the visor replaced itself, and the group zoomed away.

Sighing, Ryuu brought his rider to a rest about a foot above the ground by the gateway. He dismounted and looked back at the village, wondering if Allison would lose her temper or keep it in check. He smiled as he recalled that Bamber had been the recipient of the broken finger. Aiolos would probably be their strongest player. He tended to show a lot of his free spirit during a game, and the insults and banter usually flew out with rapid speed due to his quick tongue and wit.

Soon his vision shifted from the village. He settled back onto the seat of his bike land looked up at the clear blue sky. His thoughts moved on to his mother and the reason why she'd left him when he was born.

He closed his eyes, and a small tear ran down his cheek as he recalled the day when he found out that Jun and Chikako weren't his birth parents. About a year ago, they had sat him down in the living room and explained the events of that fateful day. The shock had hit him pretty hard. Up until that point, he had felt like the villagers looked down on him. In fact, one of the main reasons he had always worked extra hard at school was to prove his merit. However, some of the teachers frequently accused him of cheating, and he had never felt accepted by anyone but his small circle of friends. Before he got his friends, contacts, and earplugs his peers would suddenly toss loud noisemakers, blow dog whistles, sudden flashes of light, and stink bombs near him, and put miniscule sour things in his food and drink. Then laugh as he writhed on the floor protecting his ears, stumble around blinded, cover his nose with whatever was on hand as he ran from the stink, and spit out whatever was in his mouth, but he had never known why. Finally, he knew.

During the days that followed, he had questioned if he really belonged in the village and the clan. He had even made plans to leave, but when he had tried to sneak away in the middle of the night, he had discovered that a small group of supporters was waiting for him. That night, his parents and friends had persuaded him to stay, and when he had finally agreed, the entire group had smiled. Some friends had even cheered.

He brushed aside the tear. Still, even to this day, he wasn't certain that his parents had told him everything about that night. However, they had not been willing to answer any more questions, and he didn't want to appear ungrateful.

As he delved deeper into his memory, he thought back to when he first met his friends.

It was after one of the mandatory pilot classes where they all had to qualify. As per usual, he picked it up fast—and he spent most of the class getting snide remarks from both his teacher and his classmates.

When the class finished, his mind was still on the lesson. As he walked down the hall, he planned how he could improve in the next one. Then somebody shoved him from behind, knocking him down. He whipped his gaze around, teeth bared. Dulglad and his friends laughed as he attempted to get back off the ground.

That's how he first met Bryan, who came to his defense, offered him a hand, to haul him to his feet. Then, as the others hung back to watch, Ryuu launched himself at Dulglad, knocking him to the ground.

A short while later, that was how his father found him: surrounded by teachers trying to break up the fight as some students cheered it on. At that point, Ryuu was in the middle, holding Dulglad over his head like a rag doll.

Ten minutes later, he sat outside his father's office, with Dulglad hunched on the seat across from him dabbing at a bloody nose. Bryan was in the office, and Dulglad's father had also been summoned. Neither Dulglad nor Ryuu talked to one another, although they did exchange an occasional glare. Ryuu did his best to ignore the voices that seeped out through the closed door.

". . . is a menace! I told you he was too dangerous to be around the other children! He nearly killed my son!" It was Dulglad's father. "It's bad enough that you allow those half elves— but we don't even know what he is!"

"Master Iga, that's not exactly how it happened." This was Bryan's voice.

"Mr. Hunson!" snapped Dulglad's father. "I do not recall asking for you to speak!"

"And yet that is why he is here in the first place," came his father's voice. "And on that note, from what Mr. Hunson and others has told me, it was your son who started this skirmish. So maybe you should use this incident to teach your son not to provoke a fight."

His father's voice continued. "Furthermore, you know Allison and Erik lost their mother and father to the Black Dragon's forces. Fighting in the resistance, they died as heroes so that others would live. As I have reminded you, it is not up to you to select the students we admit to this school for training. Further, considering the evidence against your son, you know that he could be facing suspension for his actions in provoking Alec-Ryuu. However, I will be talking to Alec-Ryuu next. He will also have to face consequences for his actions."

There was silence for a few moments, followed by angry footsteps, and the door was thrown open. Standing there was Master Iga, who shot Ryuu a dirty look. Then he motioned for Dulglad to follow him, and the pair swept away.

"Alec-Ryuu, would you come in here?" his father said.

Sighing, Ryuu climbed to his feet and walked inside.

Before him, his father sat at his ornate desk with his elbows resting on top and his fingers interlaced. His gaze was downcast, and his head was leaning against his fingers.

"Close the door behind you Alec-Ryuu."

After doing what he was told, he walked forward to sit before his father. For a few moments, nothing but silence filled the room. Then his father finally raised his gaze to look at Ryuu.

"Well, I see you certainly are making an impression, Alec-Ryuu," he finally said.

"But Dad, I didn't—"

"I know you didn't start that fight," his father interrupted, "but the way you handled it is inexcusable." He sat back in his chair. "I know that you're only five, Alec-Ryuu, but you need to remember just how powerful you are compared to your classmates. You could have seriously hurt Dulglad, if not killed him."

His father let the statement settle for a moment. Ryuu lowered his gaze in shame at the disappointment in his father's voice.

Then his father continued. "I have something for you." He indicated the holo book laying on his desk before him. "I first set it aside because I thought you might enjoy it. Now I just hope that it will inspire you to become better than you are."

Then he turned to Bryan. "Mr. Hunson, I am hoping you will help my son learn to control his temper. Would you and your friends please look after him and find better ways to . . . vent it out?"

For a second Bryan was silent as he looked from Jun to Ryuu. Then he nodded. "Yes, Grandmaster Yamato."

Smiling, his father waved his hand. "Thank you. Both of you are dismissed."

After standing and picking up the book, Ryuu left with Bryan. They walked down the hall in silence. Then Bryan finally asked, "So . . . what's the book?"

After glancing at him, Ryuu held it up and turned on the cover. *Robin Hood.*

He was so engrossed in his thoughts that he didn't realize that the others had come back until he was poked hard on his shoulder. He jumped, fell off his rider, and looked up at Allison's smiling face as he lay on the ground.

"Ryuu, this is space command," said Aiolos. He leaned over and placed his hand over his mouth, giving his voice an echoing sound. "We're calling your head back to your body."

Ryuu laughed as he climbed to his feet and looked around at the rest of his friends. Each was carrying a bag with equipment for sky hockey. Bryan had also brought a bag for Ryuu, which he opened immediately. Inside his bag were two sets of medium and large rings; a single, larger ring; what looked like a small metal rod; and a pair of boots with red buttons on the inside of the heels.

Ryuu slipped the medium-sized rings onto his arms right on top of his biceps. The larger rings he pulled onto his legs, and they stopped just above his knees. He slipped on the largest ring, which went up to his waist. Seconds later, everything automatically shrank to fit snuggly. Finally, he slipped on another half ring around his neck and replaced his shoes with the boots. Then he turned at the sound of approaching engines. Dulglad and his friends were coming at them at top speed on their bikes.

Ryuu turned to look at his friends. He nodded. Each pressed the buttons on the rings, which expanded into full gear.

On Ryuu's arms, the rings expanded down past his elbow and encased his entire hands, including his fingers. The rings on his legs expanded up and down, but stopped just above his ankles and below the ring around his waist. Then they melded with the boots and the waist ring. The one around his waist expanded up his chest. Then it encased his shoulders and the top sections of his arms. Like before, the ring on his neck expanded up his neck, but it stopped at his hairline and chin. Finally, there was a flash of light as the force field mask activated.

When the plates were finished expanding, the friends looked like they were partly encased by some sort of armor. All of the suits turned scarlet, but because Eric was the goalie, his armor, which was thicker, included a blue rectangular shield on one arm and a large goalie glove in the other. As the friends waited, their opponents dressed in a similar fashion; their gear turned a deep green.

Slowly, the two groups gathered and faced each other.

"Ready to lose?" Dulglad asked, a cocky smile on his face.

Ryuu smiled. "You wish," he said.

Dulglad's smile turned into a deep frown. Then he stepped away and gathered his team around him.

Ryuu gathered his own team, and as they formed a circle, he placed his hand in the center. One by one, his friends placed their hands on top of his. Pumping their hands, they called out their team name as one: "LOCKSLEY!" Then they clicked their heels together.

Their boots hummed as they shot into the air, hovering about twenty feet up. Then they started to set up for the game. Eric took some balls from his glove and tossed them to either side of him; they stopped about six feet apart. They hovered for a moment, then emitted beams of light that connected, forming a goal.

Allison and Aiolos tossed a couple more balls toward him, and they hovered about another twelve feet on either side of Eric. They emitted two beams of light that connected behind Eric's goal and connected to the balls that Dulglad's friends had set up on the other end, forming the playing field. The lines appeared with multiple flashes of light as force fields formed below them and made the walls. When the arena was set, Allison, Ryuu, and Aiolos moved up to the centerline with Melinda, Dulglad, and Bamber.

When the six of them met, they all held the short sticks in their hands and activated them. The sticks lengthened, forming hockey sticks that each player gripped with both hands, except for Eric and Kade, who had goalie sticks. Allison and Aiolos took their positions as Ryuu's left and right wings as they faced off against Melinda and Bambar.

Bending his legs, Ryuu faced off against Dulglad and the two waited, eyes locked on each other, every now and then swatting each other's stick. From above fell a puck, which was coming down between Ryuu's and Dulglad's sticks. On the rebound of the puck, which hit the field, Dulglad checked Ryuu hard, taking the puck.

Ryuu slid down the field a bit then rolled back onto his feet. *I should have known they'd play dirty,* he thought as he skated after his opponent.

Bryan skated up to intercept Dulglad, but he was hooked from behind by Melinda, and Dulglad whipped past him. Eric skated out, challenging him, but he was checked hard by Bamber. Then Melinda knocked the goal a foot to the right, and Dulglad scored. Ryuu gritted his teeth in frustration as beams of light where the puck had dropped from counted the score.

As the puck soared up to where the score was displayed, the rest of Ryuu's team took their starting positions on the field. Dulglad's team continued to pull off just about every dirty trick in the book, but without a referee, they weren't called for it or forced to play fair. Soon it was 0–9.

After Dulglad scored another goal, Ryuu rolled back onto his feet, and his team gathered around him. Ryuu raised his visor and looked at his friends. They were just as angry as he was about the dirty way that Dulglad's team was playing.

"This isn't sky hockey; it's a demolition derby," Eric said behind him.

"I say we give these guys some major payback," Allison said. She brandished a fist in the air.

Ryuu pointed at her. "I'm with you, Allison, *but we're doing it by the book.* Agreed?"

All of his teammates nodded.

Dulglad and Ryuu faced off again, and this time when the puck dropped, Ryuu won the face-off. Allison checked Melinda and took the puck. She darted up the field, then drop passed the puck to Ryuu, who skated behind her. Switching positions, he dodged Babieca, skated behind their goal and then passed the puck to Aiolos.

"HONEY, I'M HOME!" he shouted. Then he fired a slap shot and scored just above Kade's raised glove.

Cheering, they reformed the lines, and an agitated Dulglad faced off against Ryuu, who was grinning. Dulglad won the face-off this time, and Ryuu stole the puck by skating up and over him on the side of the boards, with Bryan in front of him skating up the field.

Over Bryan's shoulder, Ryuu spied Melinda, Bambar, and Babieca coming at them, and Melina shouted, "He can't check all three of us!"

As they collided, Bryan did check all three of them at once, and they slid in three different directions. Ryuu's and Bryan's sticks fell in perfect sync with each other as they shot for the goal. They stopped right in front of it, and Kade stared at Bryan. Then Ryuu scored right between Bryan's and Kade's legs.

After taking their positions, again Ryuu won the face-off by knocking the puck between Dulglad's legs. He skated around him, passed to Allison, flipped over Babieca, and then swerved over and checked Melinda into the force field wall. After Ryuu received the puck, he juggled it into the air, fired a shot, and scored.

Team Locksley scored four more times in a matter of four minutes, and Dulglad's team was clearly willing to resort to any means to try to stop them. As Ryuu was skating up the field dribbling the puck between his stick, he fired a slap shot just as he was dodging around Melinda, who spun around, bent over, and flipped checked him onto his back. He heard cries of outrage as he landed hard on his back. Quickly, he raised his head to see his shot score. Curling up, he leapt to his feet and turned to face Melinda.

Bryan skated up and placed a hand on his shoulder.

"Alac—" Bryan started, but when Ryuu glared at him, he backed off.

Ryuu pushed off toward her, and she looked him dead in the eye.

"Go ahead," she muttered at him.

He glared at her, then leaned forward. "Nine," he muttered. Then he skated around her and took his position.

Dulglad took his position in front of Ryuu, a grin on his face. "Chicken," he muttered, and Ryuu cocked a grin.

Ryuu won the face-off, but he sent the puck hurtling back toward Bryan, who got it. Allison, Aiolos, and Ryuu darted back. The four of them skated back around Eric and the goal before returning to make a formation, skating up the field. They passed the puck between each other to keep Dulglad's team guessing. When Ryuu got the puck, the other three retreated and checked whoever was in his way.

It was just Ryuu and Kade now. Kade skated forward, challenging Ryuu as he progressed. Ryuu skated forward and faked a shot to Kade's left. While Kade did a wall block, Ryuu back-handed at his right. The seconds seemed to last for hours as the puck sailed forward toward the goal and Kade's glove raised. The puck missed the glove by millimeters. It sailed into the goal, and the buzzer sounded, ending the game.

Ryuu cheered, raising his hands into the air as the scoreboard flashed the score: 9–10. The rest of his team rushed forward, and they started skating in a tight circle, placing the heels of their sticks in the center.

"GOOOO LOCKLSLEY!" they shouted as one, bringing their sticks up and interlocking them as they slipped into a group hug.

When they broke apart, Ryuu turned to see that the field had dissolved after the balls had fallen to the earth. Dulglad glared at him briefly. Then he and his friends deactivated their sticks, jumped onto their bikes, and sped off.

Ryuu shook his head, knowing this latest round of the long line of clashes between the groups was far from over. In just a few hours, they would all meet again at the Academy to take their final exam.

CHAPTER 3
SAMURAI

A FTER A QUICK picnic lunch, Ryuu and his friends sat near the gateway for hours, talking about what had happened in the game and their dramatic comeback. Ryuu and Allison were reenacting his final shot when Ryuu caught sight of her watch. He grabbed her wrist and turned it so that he could see it better.

"Oh, man, my mom is going to kill me!" Ryuu darted to his rider and grabbed his surfer. "Sorry, guys, I've got to get home. Mom will kill me if I'm late."

He tossed the board forward and jumped on.

"Good luck!" Ryuu heard them call in the distance. He leaned as low as he could on his surfer, and the ground turned into one big, blurred mass.

Ryuu squinted his eyes, which stung from the rushing air that was blowing into his face. He slowed down when he soared over the village, and less than a second later, he spotted his home. Looking down, he could see his mother in the back yard, sitting on her knees with a teapot over a fire in front of her and a circle of cutting mats standing erect behind her. He zoomed above their front yard, deactivated the board, slipped off, and fell twenty feet to the ground, landing on bended knee.

The board folded up, and Ryuu lifted his hand and caught it. Then he darted up the stairs and into the house. His father wasn't home. *He must have left for school to prepare for tonight's exam,* Ryuu thought. Then he darted into his room, stripped off his shirt, and put on the clothes he would need for the test with his mother, which would be next.

As soon as he was dressed in his loose, baggy, traditional Hakama pants and his traditional Keikogi overlapping jacket, Ryuu rushed to the back door, slid it open, and walked out onto the lawn toward his mother. He sat on his knees next to her, with the teapot in front of them.

She was dressed like him, with her hair tied back. She had placed a katana sword on her hip, and her eyes were closed.

She said, "Right on time, Alac-Ryuu, although I thought I heard you in a little rush in the house."

Ryuu smiled at her, lowering his gaze down to the sash that was folded neatly at his knees and the katana at his right side.

"You know what to do," she said.

First he placed his hands on the sash and bowed to her. As he sat up, he picked up the sash with the same movement. Then he unfolded it and tied it over his eyes.

Next, he picked up the sword. He lifted it with both hands while he bowed his head, then he tucked it into the sash around his waist and waited.

After a moment, the water in the kettle began to whistle, and Ryuu lifted it from its holder and placed it gently on a clay coaster. He then took two cups and went through a traditional tea ceremony with his eyes covered. When he was finished, he handed one cup to his mother, picked up his own, and waved a hand over it. Then he drank.

When they were finished with their tea, Ryuu put the cup down, and his hand shot up and caught her shuto knife hand before it could make contact with his face.

"Good. Move onto the next stage," she said.

Ryuu leaned forward and put his toes under him. Then he pushed himself onto his feet and walked around the small fire. He stopped after a few steps and turned around on his heel, facing the way he'd come. He took a deep breath, then gripped his sword and drew it slowly.

Next, he gripped the sword with both hands and slashed the air at ten different spots around him. Each of his attacks he struck differently, using an upward, side, or downward slash. Before he faced the way he came, he sheathed his sword and stood straight as an arrow, waiting.

Without warning, he drew his sword, and there was a clash of steel on steel as his mother began her attack. He brought his sword down in a wide arch, and as he stepped back, keeping low, he listened to what was around him with his ears and with his feet. He turned slightly and parried another blow.

They exchanged a few more blows with each other. As he turned lightly to the left, he brandished his sword so fast he knew it must look like nothing more than a blur. After ducking and quickly turning, he spun around and parried another blow. Then he ran the blunt edge up to elbow level and pressed it against something. He twisted it a little to persuade his attacker to stop.

After a moment, he withdrew his sword, sheathed it, and stood straight, one hand on the sheath. He then felt his mother stand in front of him, and they bowed to each other. He stood straight as he felt and heard her move away from him. A moment later, he drew his sword in a flash and felt something impact on the blade. He shifted the sword and blocked again and again, each something impacted his sword blade.

After the last blow, he sheathed his sword and waited. Soon he felt her coming. She grabbed him around the neck, and he was forced to bend over. He grabbed her ankles and stood straight, which made her fall back against the ground, knocking the wind out of her. Still holding onto her, Ryuu twisted around, sat on her, and placed her leg in a lock until she patted the ground three times.

He rolled off her and stood straight, with one hand on his sword. He waited for her to make her move. When she came at him again from behind, he rammed his elbow into her gut. Then he grabbed her wrist with one hand, grasped her under her armpit with the other, threw her over his shoulder, and twisted her arm around into a lock. Once more, she patted the ground, and he rolled off her again, rose to his feet, and waited.

He suddenly felt her come at him again from behind. This time she managed to put him a blood choke. He got low on his knees and gripped her arm, knowing he didn't have long before he was out. He got down on one knee, threw his hips forward, and flipped her over his shoulder hard onto the ground. Then he stood straight, waiting for her to make a move again.

This time she came at him from the front, and he grabbed her hand. She twisted his arm around as she stepped behind him. Locking out her wrist, he brought her back, flipped her onto her side, and punched down a centimeter from her face. He stood straight and waited for her next attack.

This time it came from his front, and as she grabbed his collar, he grabbed hers, and she threw him into the air, twisting around. He grabbed her neck with his legs and brought her down hard. As he held onto her arm, she landed on her back, and he held her wrist in an arm bar. He twisted wrist, and put her in a double lock. She patted the ground again, and he rolled back onto his feet.

"Remove the blindfold, Alac-Ryuu," said his mother.

He slipped it off and looked at her in front of him, then at the cutting mats around the two of them. They were all now six inches shorter than they had been before. Some of them had been cut at various angles, with shattered arrows around them. He couldn't help but smile as he looked back at her. Then they walked back to the fire.

They knelt across from each other again.

"Recite the seven virtues and their meaning," his mother commanded.

Ryuu breathed deeply.

"One, *Gi*: the right decision, taken with equanimity; the right attitude; the truth. When we must die, we must die. Rectitude.

"Two, *Yu*: bravery tinged with heroism.

"Three, *Jin*: universal love; benevolence toward humanity; compassion.

"Four, *Rei*: right action—a most essential quality; courtesy.

"Five, *Makoto*: utter sincerity; truthfulness.

"Six, *Melyo*: honor and glory.

"Seven, *Chugo*: devotion; loyalty."

His mother held her stern gaze on him for a long moment, and then she smiled from ear to ear. "Well done, Alac-Ryuu, very well done. When we started, you were my student to my family's style. Now you've earned the right to call yourself Samurai." She bowed to him.

Ryuu smiled back at her. "Thank you, my mother." He bowed to her.

A half hour later, Ryuu was sitting at the coffee table dressed in black. In front of him were weapons and tools he would need for the test with his father that night. He looked at the clock every few seconds, taking deep breaths. His mother soon came out of the kitchen, another cup of tea in her hand. He was far too nervous to eat dinner, and he was glad to see that she understood that.

She placed the tea in front of him, and he picked it up and drank deeply.

"Relax, honey," she said. "If you perform like you did earlier, you'll be fine."

He put the cup back down and looked at her. "You wouldn't be singing the same tune if you were in my place, Mom." He looked at the clock again. "It's time."

One by one, he picked up the weapons and tools from the table and slipped them into their proper place. He picked up the remaining pieces of his uniform, pulled the balaclava over his head, and tucked it under his jacket. The last piece, a long strip of cloth, he tied over the spot where his mouth would have shown, and when he was finished, the only part of his body that showed was his eyes.

His weapons were a Kumai knife carrier, which was strapped to his upper right leg, and a shuriken, a star-shaped weapon with projecting blades, which was contained in a carrier that was strapped to his other leg. He slipped the three-pronged, bladed-edged Sais to their sheaths, which were connected to the Kumai knives and, shuriken carrier, and buckled them in. He then slipped the chucks into the antigravity belt around his waist, which the carriers were strapped to.

The last weapons he picked up were his sword, quiver, and bow. He quickly tied the three to his back. Feeling like his limbs had turned to lead, he faced his mother and smiled behind his mask as best he could. Then he left through the back door as silent as the dead, and after sprinting across the lawn, he leapt into the trees.

A ways in, Ryuu stashed some of his weapons away in a tree hollow. Then he leapt away, memorizing the area so he could find them again.

For the next few minutes, Ryuu leapt from tree to tree. He was so quiet, the animals gave no warning of his presence, even when Ryuu landed next to an owl. Ryuu looked at creature as it turned his head. Then it gave a small hoot and flew off.

Ryuu traced the owl's path as it moved across the clear night sky. The moon was full, and the stars were bright. He thought, *it has begun.*

CHAPTER 4
NINJA

RYUU CREPT THROUGH the forest in the late hours of the night, keeping his knees bent and cross walking with his hands out for balance. As he walked, he kept looking left and right. He saw only trees, but he knew more was out there. After taking a few more steps, he froze and dropped lower. In the moonlight, he ran a finger along a wire that was almost invisible in the gloom.

Making up his mind, he took a few steps back, and from his carrier he drew a four-pointed star shuriken. He stepped behind a tree. After a moment, he whipped around and threw the star, which cut the wire. A log swung down lengthwise and past him, and he exhaled deeply, relieved that he had not been standing in front of it.

He leapt up and wall-jumped up to a tree branch. Then he ducked down, keeping a sharp watch on his surroundings. Quick as a flash, he drew his sword when a black-clad figure approached. Then he spun around, and blocked his opponent's sword, which was aimed at his head. As he pushed the sword away, he fell off the tree, flipped around, and landed on his feet. When he looked up, this opponent was gone.

He stated moving away, as quiet as the dead, hunting what he couldn't see or hear. Suddenly, he stopped. His eyes darted to his right. He leapt up on a tree branch and reached into his carrier. He whipped around and flung a four-pointed metal star. It sailed about twenty feet away, where one of the blades became embedded in a tree right in front of another black-clad figure. This figure, who had a staff across his back, stopped dead in his tracks and stared at the star as he was coming around the tree.

Quietly running along the branch until he reached the end, Ryuu leapt from it, throwing a flying sidekick. The other figure looked at him and then ducked under the kick, which put a foot-shaped hole in the tree. Before the staffed figure could retaliate, Ryuu spun around in the air and threw a sidekick to his head.

Ryuu flipped backwards back onto his feet. They landed and assumed fighting stances. When they circled each other, the staff bearer pulled out his staff and twirled it above his head and behind him, one hand extended outwards. Ryuu recognized it and took a closer look at the clad figure in front of him.

"I'm a warrior chosen by a creature that's connected to all four elements of life," Ryuu said.

The staff bearer got out of his fighting stance. "I'm a warrior bound by a code to protect the weak, abused, and the innocent," he said. It was Bryan.

Bryan put his staff away, and the two grasped hands. Then he pointed at his friend. "Remind me to kick your butt later, Ryuu," he said.

Ryuu patted him on the shoulder.

"Fat chance, Bryan, my friend. Now let's finish this examination," he said, and the two headed out together.

After traveling for almost ten minutes, they stopped and examined their surroundings.

"You take cover down here. I'll take the trees, LJ," Ryuu said.

Even in the dark, Ryuu could see his friend roll his eyes. "Sure thing, Robin. Good luck," he said. Then he moved off.

Ryuu watched him go. Then he leapt up into the trees and

started following Bryan by jumping from branch to branch. He made a brief stop on an oak with a large hole, and, reaching in, he pulled out a quiver full of arrows and an unstrung bow in a strapped leather tube. He placed both items over his shoulder and continued to follow Bryan as the two looked for their target.

They traveled like that for another ten minutes. Then Bryan was attacked by their target. As he started to fight back, Ryuu leapt from his hiding spot and double- kicked the attacker in the chest. Using the momentum of the kick, the figure flipped back, pressed a button on his belt, and then dived directly into the ground.

Ryuu and Bryan stood back-to-back, looking down at the ground, with weapons drawn at the ready.

"We've got a mole on our hands," Bryan said.

"Well, you know what they say, bro. Fight fire with fire."

They looked at each other and nodded. Then they quickly pressed the buttons on their own belts and sank into the ground, following their target.

A few seconds later, the three figures burst back to the surface with an ear-splitting sound that reverberated through the forest like a train crash. Their target pressed another button on its belt and started running through the air. Seeing this, Ryuu and Bryan mimicked his moves and followed him as fast as they could.

As they were catching up, there was a faint buzzing sound like a bee, and the figure dodged onto a tree branch, barely escaping a pair of Sais. Ryuu couldn't tell who had launched them until Allison and Aiolos leapt into view onto a branch to the side of their target. As Allison passed by, she retrieved her Sai swords and twirled them in her hands. Then she got into a fighting stance, with one Sai reversed.

Aiolos drew a pair of numchucks, and they quickly turned into a blur of motion like the prop of an antique plane: left, right, up, and down. Next he grasped both ends in his hands, ready for what was to come. Ryuu drew his bow, fitted an arrow to it, and placed their target in his sights.

Their target looked at the two groups—one in front and one to the side of him—and he took a step back.

"I wouldn't keep moving if I were you," a fifth person told him. Ryuu recognized the voice. It was Erik.

Their target whipped around and stared at Erik, who was standing on a branch, bow in hand, with an arrow sighted at the target. The figure looked from Erik to Aiolos to Allison to Bryan to Ryuu. Before anything else could happen, Ryuu heard a faint rustling, and his nostrils were filled with a pungent odor when the wind changed.

He turned his eyes up just in time to see a small orb- like object drop between them. Then went off. He doubled over, eyes shut in agonizing pain, as a blinding flash of light and a deafening sound filled his head.

He twisted and turned as his ears rang with the blast of noise. While it felt like his eyes were being stung by white hot needles

Then he felt a rush of air. Before he could right himself, his side slammed against something hard that sent him spinning. Twice more he collided with hard objects— first in the back and then in the head. Finally he came to a hard stop on the unforgiving ground.

As his body rang with pain, he curled up into a fetal position. ears and eyes still covered as best he could.

He couldn't tell how much had passed, but when he finally was able to open his eyes, he saw nothing but blackness. Suddenly he became aware of rough, gloved hands shaking him hard.

"RYUU! RYUU!" someone was screaming. "RYUU ANSWER US!"

"Stop shouting! My ears hurt enough as it is," he whimpered.

"Oh, thank the gods." Bryan's voice was filled with relief.

"Anything else we should know?" came Allison's voice.

"I can't see," Ryuu answered. "And my head feels like a starship landed on it. What was that?"

He heard Aiolos speak next. "That's not surprising considering that blow to the head you took falling. And to answer that question, it was a flash bang. Our target booked it when you fell."

"Erik, help me to sit him up," Allison said, and he was gently shifted into position. "Ryuu, I'm shining a light in your eye. Do you see it?"

Ryuu just stared ahead. The blackness seemed never ending. "Nothing," he answered.

"Gods above!" Allison cursed. "I wish we took more than basic first aid. But from what I can tell from your pupils, you might have a slight concussion."

"You guys wait here. I'll get help." Brian said.

"NO!"

Ryuu heard everyone turn toward him.

"Ryuu you need—" Allison started.

"I know who did it." They fell silent. "I smelled him. It was Dulglad."

"Bastard!" Brian barked. "His father must have told him our grid, and they set this up to ensure we fail!"

"Not you, me!" Ryuu growled. He climbed to his feet. "And I'm not going to quit! They are not going to stop me from graduating!"

"But Ryuu, you can't see," Erik said. "How are you going to continue?"

"I can hear, and I can smell!" he hissed. Then he followed a scent to a tree and felt for a branch. "You guys will be my eyes. We all used flash bangs in training; we know this is temporary..." He turned, holding the branch to keep himself steady.

"Ryuu, that was in daylight, and it took half an hour for your sight to return," Brian said. "And that isn't counting—"

"I can do this!" Ryuu snapped. "Our target is still in the area! Get me up high enough and I can help you find him! You know we need every advantage we can get!"

For the next few seconds, Ryuu could almost hear the silent argument between them.

Then he heard Allison step forward. She wrapped her arm around his waist and put his arm over her shoulder. "Hang on," she muttered, and with her help, they climbed higher and higher into the trees.

When they reached a suitable spot, Allison settled him on a branch. She helped him knell down, gripping the branch in his hand.

Focusing on what his mother had taught him, he turned his head left and right to catch every sound around him while his ears slowly began to stop ringing. He took several deep sniffs, and the smells of the forest flooded him.

For the next ten minutes, he remained like that, going through the same movements. His aim was to pull that one particular scent and sound to help his friends.

As the minutes ticked by, the urgency to find their target grew rapidly, along with his rising panic that he would not be able to stop his friends from being dragged down with him.

Just as the tension reached a boiling point, he froze. After taking two more sniffs, he whipped out a kunai knife. Spinning in a new direction, he hissed, "That way!"

Ryuu heard the others move forward. Carefully drawing back against the trunk of the tree. Ryuu raised his gaze up ward as he focused on the return of his senses.

Moments later he faintly heard, "You learned to work as a team; now it's time to work alone." Then he heard the breaking of glass, and he knew the target was gone.

When his friends returned, they cheered their success in the first part of this final test of their training.

"Erik, you're a genius!" Allison said.

"About time you admitted it, Allison."

"Did you see the look in his eyes when he realized we had herded him?"

"Hey," Bryan interjected, "me and Ryuu should get the credit for that! I did the herding, and Ryuu sniffed him out!"

"True," Ryuu said, "but this isn't over yet. We now have to accomplish that alone. We can't rely on each other as a team anymore. From here on out, it's one on one."

The group's sense of jubilation was quickly replaced with an air of nervousness.

"You really know how to kill a mood there, Ryuu," Bryan said.

Ryuu shrugged. "I'm just saying how it is. I don't mean to sound negative. Now let's head up the mountain to the Academy and finish what we started tonight. That is— after my sight returns."

CHAPTER 5
JOURNEY TO THE ACADEMY

I T TOOK NEARLY an hour for his sight to return. When it did, the group spent the next thirty minutes jumping from branch to branch, moving further up the mountain. Ryuu felt like his legs were made of lead. Eventually, he stopped and looked up a ridge that was covered by the forest's oldest trees at the mountain's highest points. A waterfall flowed out of the ridge, into a pool in front of them.

Ryuu and his friends dropped down to the ground. All around them, the blades of grass swayed in the night air.

He looked at his friends and nodded. "Okay, let's do it."

They darted along the edge of the water until they reached the side of the waterfall. After a quick look around, Ryuu pressed on a medium-sized rock. Suddenly they were standing on the edge of the mountain, higher up still, in the forest region of a location that only Ryuu's father, the grandmaster, knew. In front of them was the Gold Dragon Academy, which was built in the Japanese castle style with pillars and sloping roofs that didn't rise above the cover of the trees.

The Academy, founded centuries ago, was now run by Ryuu's father, who was dedicated to training a new generation of warriors. For centuries, the Black Dragon had failed to find it, and now the

Academy also stood as a symbol of hope, especially for members of the Resistance, which many of the students joined after the completion of their training.

Ryuu and his friends stood there for a moment, just looking at it.

Aiolos folded his arms and said, "And to think that after tonight some of us may never see this place again."

Ryuu nodded and turned to his friends. "What are your plans for after tonight?"

Allison said, "Straight to the Resistance for me." Then she added, "That's after I take care of a few things here."

Erik said, "I follow my sister."

"Same here," Bryan agreed.

That left Aiolos. "Me, too. What about you, Ryuu?"

At first, he remained silent. "I don't know," he finally said. "My father has been asked to start training his replacement. I may stay and work to take his place here. Or else I... just might strike out on my own."

"What?" Allison demanded. "Why?"

Sighing, Ryuu looked away. "Look, I've been here for my whole life, and I'm still having trouble fitting in." He turned back to them. "Do you really think that—beyond you guys—I'd find more acceptance among their ranks? Or the same derision?"

After a few beats of silence, Allison put a hand on his shoulder. "We'll miss you, bro," she said. "No matter what you decide. We'll always be there for each other."

He smiled at them. "Well, you'll know where to find me, hopefully. Let's go!"

Once again, Ryuu took the lead, and they ran through the woods toward the Academy as fast as they could. He kept his hands back for balance as he leaned forward. They soon reached a narrow stone path, which had stone walls on either side that stood about ten feet high. They twisted and turned with the passage and leapt or flipped over obstacles as they darted along.

Eventually they approached a pit in the ground and leapt over it. One by one they grabbed a pole, which was embedded into the solid stone, and flipped over the pole a couple times before launching forward onto a platform set into a stone wall. Darting around the corner, they came to a wall and wall-jumped up to another platform. Then they darted forward again down the passage toward a series of ropes.

They each took out a four-pointed shuriken and hurled it to the side. The ropes started to shoot up, and they leapt up after them, hands outstretched. When they grabbed the ropes, they shot up like rockets through the stone tunnel.

At the top of the tunnel, where the pulley system ended, they released the ropes. One by one, they were launched into the air. Ryuu tucked his legs close as he shot into the sky over the same wide ravine where they had raced their sky riders earlier. The ravine separated the two woods on either side and the Academy. He pressed the buttons on his anti-gravbelt as he soared through the air. Then he flipped around as they started to come down in the courtyard of the school, and his descent slowed.

At the end of the flip, he grabbed the branch of a tree on the edge of the ravine, swung under it, and flipped off it. He landed on one knee in the middle of a stone path in front of the main wooden gates and remained in that position, scanning the area with his eyes. The courtyard was almost full.

His friends landed beside him.

"Looks like we're almost the last ones here," Allison muttered.

"Are you that surprised?" Erik asked her.

"No, not really."

"We're just too good," Aiolos said. "Despite almost being sabotaged."

"Aiolos, don't get overconfident."

"Oh, come on, Bryan, don't kill the mood."

"Aiolos, be serious."

"Ryuu, even you have to admit we're the best in the school."

"Yes, but that doesn't mean we should boast, especially since half the teachers here think I cheated my way to the top," Ryuu said. Then the group fell silent.

For half an hour, they remained that way, down on one knee and hand, waiting for more teams that had passed to arrive. Eventually, fifteen more teams arrived just inside the time frame. Ryuu looked over at Dulglad's group and noted with some satisfaction that his group looked beaten up. When all the teams were assembled, he heard the sound of grinding metal, and the giant wooden doors began to open.

Bit by bit the doors opened, and standing inside the doors was Ryuu's father, the grandmaster. He was wearing the traditional red grandmaster kimono with the lotus symbol of the clan on both of his shoulders. When the doors were all the way open, he stepped forward and surveyed the students as he walked down the line, looking each team member in the face.

The last team he checked was Ryuu's. He started with Aiolos and worked his way down until he finally reached Ryuu. Unable to resist, Ryuu glanced at his father, and the two looked each other in the eye for a split second before Ryuu dropped his gaze to the ground.

Jun smiled, walked back to the entrance, and looked at the students. He spread his arms wide and said, "I congratulate each and every one of you on a job well done on this part of the exams. Out of all the teams, only one failed to pass this part of your final examination. But for those who have passed, I would like to say that I'm proud of each and every one of you for your notable effort.

"Now it's time for the second—and most important—part of your final examination. This will test all your personal knowledge as a ninja, and the passing of this test will bring an end to your training here. For some of you who have reached the age of eighteen, the completion of this test will mean not only the end of your lives here at the Academy, but also the end of your lives here on this planet as you journey forth into the unknown."

Ryuu briefly looked at his friends. He would miss each one of them.

Then his father continued.

"I'll call you forward one at a time, and you'll proceed inside for the examination. Take this warning seriously. Be careful which path you choose. I wish you all luck, and let the second part of the examination begin!"

He stepped back into the shadows and vanished completely.

CHAPTER 6
THE FINAL EXAM

ONE BY ONE, their names were called.

"Allison Cromnae."

Allison stood in a flash. She glanced at her friends, darted into the Academy, and soon was out of sight. For a little more than an hour, they others remained where they were, waiting for her to pass or fail while the moon and stars slowly crept their way across the sky. Then . . .

"Erick Cromnae."

Over the course of several hours, the students in the courtyard lessened one by one until only Ryuu remained. Then, at long last, . . .

"Alec-Ryuu Jun Yamamoto."

Ryuu shot to his feet, stepped inside, and whipped around when he heard the gates start to close behind him. When they were completely closed, he was encased in darkness. After his eyes adjusted, he looked around through the gloom. Ahead of him were three tall, open doors.

He took a breath and quickly decided to try the middle door. As he approached the frame, a thick stone wall slammed down. He jumped back a little, surprised, then looked at the door to the left.

You'd think after almost thirteen years I'd be used to this, he thought. *Dad said we were supposed to pick which way we wanted to go.* He was about to enter through the doorway when he heard a loud crack above him.

He quickly turned back and leapt. Then he rolled back as another wall shot down and hit home where he'd been standing just a second ago. Breathing hard, he turned to look at the only unblocked passage.

Why this way? Probably the hardest of the three and the most dangerous. The teachers are probably trying to get me to quit or to prove that I cheated, he thought, and walked toward it.

He took a step over the threshold then jerked back, looking up, but nothing came down. He then took a deep breath and moved forward. When he was about twenty feet in, he stopped and looked back. The wall still hadn't fallen. Then he looked forward toward the pitch-black hall.

"I'm not going to quit," he muttered and started down it.

He walked down the hall in the darkness, his back to the wall with his hands hovering about an inch or two from it. Approaching the end, he peeked around the corner, eyes darting left and right, hearing and seeing nothing.

Something's not right. This doesn't feel like a test, he thought, but he had little choice other than to continue down the hall.

Through the darkness, he took a couple of steps forward. Suddenly, he leapt forward as, one right after other, sharp pointed rods shot out of the wall and into the opposite wall. He wall-jumped, flipped, rolled, and did everything in between to avoid being impaled by the poles.

He breathed hard, then ducked and rolled forward as a foot slammed into the wall where his head had just been. He whipped around as someone dressed like him stepped out of a concealed room and looked at him for a second, then crouched. Ryuu mimicked his movements in a flash.

Less than a second later, Ryuu threw a kick behind him, and it connected to another attacker, who was coming from the rear, followed by others. Ryuu then threw a front kick to the opponent in front of him, knocking the attacker back a couple steps. Next, he spun around, blocking a blow with his knee. He then jumped and then used his leg to nail the attacker with a kick to the head. As he spun to the ground, Ryuu grabbed the attacker around the neck with a one-arm chokehold. His opponent's face turned down and he gave it a quick jerk.

Ryuu heard a snapping sound from the neck. He released him, and he fell to the floor, twitching. Ryuu then dropped down and swept the legs out from under the opponent beside him. Next, as that attacker was sitting up, Ryuu's leg swung forward in a blur of motion, nailing him across the face and sending him face-first into the floor. Ryuu rolled over him, pulled his head back, and struck him hard in the base of the neck with a shuto.

Ryuu then rolled forward and turned to face the last attacker, who climbed to his feet and stared at him. The two crouched in fighting stances, and Ryuu's attacker fired a hook kick to the head. Ryuu ducked under it, then blocked a roundhouse from the other leg, and his attacker took a step back after blocking a roundhouse from Ryuu.

For another long moment, they faced each other. Without warning, Ryuu's attacker hopped forward and threw a roundhouse. Ryuu blocked it, and his attacker threw a turning sidekick, which Ryuu blocked before throwing his own. His attacker blocked that kick and then threw a roundhouse, followed by another hook kick, which Ryuu blocked. Then Ryuu leapt up, nailing his attacker with a crescent kick to the head.

His opponent was knocked to the ground, but he rolled back onto his feet, and they faced off again. Ryuu threw a roundhouse, which his attacker blocked. When his opponent brought his foot down, Ryuu threw a punch, which his attacker sidestepped, driving his elbow into Ryuu's gut. To Ryuu's dismay, his attacker got a few more punches in before he could back off.

His attacker came after him again, throwing punches that Ryuu blocked. Then Ryuu nailed his opponent with a palm strike to the face. After that move, he whipped around, nailing the attacker with a backhand and knocking him off his feet. Seconds later, his attacker rolled back onto his feet and threw a front kick, which Ryuu grabbed. He then lifted his opponent off his feet, slamming him back onto the ground.

The next time his attacker was back on his feet, they circled each other. This his opponent threw a punch at Ryuu's head. Ryuu blocked it, took hold of it, spun around, and flipped his foe onto his back. In a flash, his assailant was back on his feet. He spun around and kicked Ryuu's lower leg.

Ryuu gritted his teeth behind his mask as he struggled to stay standing, and his attacker threw a second kick. Ryuu blocked it, and as his enemy threw a third kick, he countered with a sidekick to his attacker's other knee. His attacker went down hard but was back on his feet in a flash.

His opponent tried to nail Ryuu with a high sidekick to the head, but Ryuu dropped down and nailed a second sidekick to the same knee. His attacker went back down, and Ryuu was back on his feet as his enemy got back up again. They stared at each other for half a second. Then Ryuu's attacker threw another punch.

Ryuu blocked it, then caught it, and nailed his attacker with a backhand across the face before driving his gut into his rising knee. Ryuu forced his face up and nailed it with a palm strike to the face, immediately followed by a second one, driving him back before jumping up and nailing a second jumping crescent kick. His attacker hurtled to the ground before slowly climbing to his feet.

This time his attacker threw another punch, which Ryuu spun around, driving his elbow into his attacker's back. Ryuu nailed him with a second elbow to the gut before putting him in a one-arm chokehold. His attacker struggled a little, but Ryuu turned on the spot so they stood back to back Ryuu still held onto his attacker's head on his shoulder with both hands.

Ryuu felt his foe's feet dangle against his calves as he struggled to free himself from Ryuu's grasp. Then Ryuu jerked his attacker's head back, heard a snap, and let him go. He felt his attacker slide down his back onto the floor, where he didn't move.

Ryuu turned and looked down at the three assailants at his feet. Then he bent down and removed the masks from the two who were not moving. Beneath each mask was a black piece of dark metal, and Ryuu recognized that this was where a holographic face would have been displayed before he had snapped each neck, cutting the power.

"Combat Bots," Ryuu muttered, before he moved on to the one who was still twitching.

He pulled back the mask and was glad to see the holographic human face. Then he lifted its right arm up with no resistance. He pulled its sleeve back and opened one of its access command ports. As soon as it was all the way up, the screen lit up, and Ryuu frowned at the red words printed on it.

KILL ALEC-RYUU

He pressed a button. A data strip popped out near the programming port, and he slipped it into his gauntlet before darting down the hall. At the next corner, he flattened himself against the wall and waited. Suddenly he threw a ridge hand, nailing a Combat Bot in the throat.

Before the Combat Bot could get its bearings, Ryuu grabbed it around its head and flipped it onto its back. Before the Bot could make a counterattack, Ryuu, quick as a flash, dropped down and grabbed it by the head. He twisted it hard to the side. He heard it snap, and when it didn't move after that, he continued.

He now knew that this was planned to be more than a final test of his skill. This was a hunt, and he was the prize buck of the herd.

Well this is one head that won't be mounted over their fireplace, he thought. Then he continued to move silently.

After the third corner he passed without any incident, he started to get a little edgy, so he stopped and looked around. He drew one of his Kunai knives from his leg sheath, twirled it around his finger by the ring at the end, and slashed a big X on the wall. He then continued onward. Ten minutes later, he stopped again, looked around, and slammed his fist into the wall.

As he stared at the giant X, he realized that he was standing exactly where he'd been ten minutes ago. He looked around the bend, drew some of his Tonki metal balls from a pocket on his belt, and tossed them down the hallway. He watched the hallway for a few seconds, but nothing happened. Then he drew a couple more and tossed them behind him. Still nothing.

A second later, he heard a small sound no louder than a mouse scurrying across the floor. Without much surprise, he watched as the opposite corner at the end of the hall began to turn. A few seconds later, it had opened a hall that headed in a completely different direction.

Ryuu waited a moment. Then, confident, he stepped out into the middle of the hall but froze at the threshold. *Why do I have the feeling everything is completely safe?* he thought.

Unable to shake the feeling, he reached inside another belt pocket, pulled out a handful of powder, and held it close to his mouth. After taking a deep breath, he blew the power down the hall, and his eyes went wide with what he saw. From the ceiling to the floor—and every other angle in between—were lines of tightly grouped lasers.

There's no pattern to them, and they're too close together to slip by them, he thought. He was even more worried about what they might trigger.

Ryuu darted forward at full speed, and a second later, right behind him, lasers started firing from one wall to the other. He raced ahead of the laser fire as he rounded the corner. After running almost flat out for almost twenty minutes, dodging around corners and doing everything he could to keep ahead of the laser fire, he saw something that almost brought him to a stop.

Ahead, a section of the ceiling and floor was rising up and down, sealing him in. He ran as fast as his legs would carry him, and when the two walls were about a foot apart, he dived forward, hands thrust out in front of him, and sailed between them, his feet barely clearing the gap just before they slammed close. He rolled on the ground, whipped around, and looked at the solid wall behind him, breathing hard in relief.

"That, I doubt, is part of the testing," he muttered. Then he stood straight and continued on his way at a brisk run.

At the next turn, he flattened himself against the wall and pulled out a star shuriken. Using one of the blades as a mirror, he checked the hall before dashing down it. After the next turn, he finally relaxed. There was a sliding Japanese door at the end of the hall. He slipped out a shuriken, hurled it halfway down the hallway, and watched as it planted itself into the stone floor.

A split second later, what looked like an axe swung out of the wall and planted itself in the opposite wall.

Ryuu shook his head. "This is getting kind of freaky," he said aloud. Then he walked forward and picked up the shuriken.

He stepped around the axe, slid back the door, and stepped into an area that resembled an old-fashioned, Dojo-decked room. One of his teachers was sitting on his knees, a sheathed katana on the floor at his side, facing the opposite wall. Even from the back, he was recognizable.

As Ryuu slid the door closed behind him, the man shifted.

"I see you've made it this far. Impressive for a cheat," he said.

The man stood up, picking up the katana, and turned to face Ryuu with his usual sneer. Ryuu said nothing but unslung his bow and slipped a couple of arrows from the quiver. Ahead, his teacher, in a ring of steel, drew his sword and dropped the sheath at his side.

"Tonight you'll be exposed as the cheat that you are," he said. The man got into a fighting stance and charged forward.

As Ryuu fired all the arrows, which were blocked by his teacher's sword, his teacher closed the distance between them. Ryuu ducked when the man reached out with his sword to swipe Ryuu's neck. As soon as the sword cleared, quicker than a flash, Ryuu hooked him around the neck with the string of the bow. His teacher turned to face him as his teacher's momentum pulled the bowstring.

Ryuu looked him in the eye for half a second before letting the bow go, and it slammed into his teacher's face, knocking him off his feet.

"Cheat that" Ryuu mocked, standing over him.

Ryuu look at his teacher, who now had a massive bump on his forehead and a bloody, broken nose. He then picked up his bow and started to leave. Stopping in mid-step, he looked back at his teacher. Quickly making up his mind, he returned to his teacher's side and drew one of his kunai knives.

He used it to cut a section from his teacher's clothes. He folded up the cloth, dabbed the blood from the man's nose, then took some herbs from a secret pocket. He crushed the juices out of them, poured them onto the cloth, and placed it on his teacher's forehead before silently leaving the room through the sliding door on the opposite wall.

Ryuu looked down the hall and smiled when he saw the night sky light the opening at the end of it. Then he heard a loud grinding sound. He darted forward as fast as he could as the walls began closing in on him. He knew that if he didn't make it out in time, he would be crushed like a grape between two fingers. He felt his heart beating under his ribs as he ran flat out. The walls continued to get closer and closer, threatening to turn him into a pancake.

His muscles burned from the constant usage, and he could

almost hear them screaming at him to stop. He silently gave himself a pep talk.

Come on Alec-Ryuu Jun Yamamoto. You're almost through this! You can rest all you want when this is over, but right now, you've got to run or be killed!

The gap became smaller and smaller, but somehow he went faster.

When he was barely a few yards from the exit, with his pumping elbows scraping the walls, he leapt forward, spinning hands and arms outstretched. His fingertips were clear . . . his elbows were clear . . . the walls were inches from his face . . . his head was clear . . . his chest and stomach were clear . . . he felt the walls barely scraping his knees. The walls slammed home just as the tips of his toes cleared, he was out, and he rolled onto his back, completely out of breath.

He lay there for a moment, looking up at the night sky. Then, uncontrollably, he started to laugh. He could not control his laughter even as he heard running footsteps coming his way. He was still laughing when several masked faces appeared in his vision, peering down at him.

"What's up with him?" Allison said.

"He seems to be showing a loss of motor control," Eric answered.

"What?" Bryan said.

"He's lost it."

"No he's just . . . giddy," Aiolos said.

"Hey, Aiolos." Ryuu reached up and grabbed Aiolos's arm, still laughing.

"What?"

"Have you ever seen such a beautiful night?" His laughing increased.

Aiolos looked at Eric and said, "No, you're right on the button, Eric. He's definitely lost it."

This only made Ryuu laugh even louder.

CHAPTER 7
THE DRAGON KNIGHTS

RYUU WAS STILL laughing when they helped him sit up, and he saw his father examining the wall that he'd just run out of. When Ryuu was finally able to calm himself down, he stood and his father came over. Jun glanced at Ryuu for a second, then back at the wall, then at Ryuu again.

Jun then jabbed a thumb back at the wall. "Did you just come from there?" he demanded.

Ryuu nodded, and his father took a couple steps back in shocked surprise.

"*Alec-Ryuu Jun Yamamoto, what possessed you to go that way?*" he snapped. "That was the course I took when I was tested for the position of grandmaster!"

Everyone stared as he continued. "And for that matter, who the heck left it open? It was supposed to be closed for the testers tonight!"

Ryuu shrugged and removed his mask. "I didn't have much of a choice in the matter. I was going to go for the opening in the middle when a solid stone wall stopped me. It almost crushed me, too."

"Damn," Aiolos muttered. "First it was that flash bang, and now this."

"FLASH BANG!" his father barked, whipping around, and Ryuu shot Aiolos a hard look. "Would one of you tell me exactly what is going on tonight?"

During the next five minutes, Ryuu explained everything that had happened. When he was finished, his father just stared at him.

"*Incredible.* That's never happened before. And I never imagined that Shuji would go to such lengths!"

Then he asked to see the data strip that Ryuu had taken from the Combat Bot.

Ryuu bent his right wrist back, and with two fingers from his left hand, he pulled the strip from under his gauntlet. His father took the strip and then bowed to him. Alec returned the gesture and then his father walked way, the strip clenched in his fist.

After Jun left the area, Ryuu's friends put their hands on his shoulders and back. They each congratulated him on getting through the course in one piece.

"Man, I can see why that's only for Grandmaster Status testing," Erik said. "No safety features, no chance of stealth entry, and you always have to be on the move, with an outcome of pass or die."

Ryuu nodded. "You don't have to tell me. What'd you guys do?"

Allison glanced at him as they walked in the same direction his father had taken. "We took the middle passage. It was pretty much a snatch-and grab-mission, whereas yours sounds more like an assassination," she said.

Ryuu nodded. "Yeah, and the only way to get in and out was being a one-man army and a tight squeeze."

Ryuu slipped his mask back on as the rest of the class came into view. They were lined up in two rows. All of the teams were sitting back on their heels, facing a low stage that was about ten feet from the first row of students. Across the opening, banners with Japanese lettering hung from the pillars.

They stepped inside the walled courtyard, and Ryuu's eyes

traveled over the brightly colored banners that had been put up for the graduation ceremony.

They made their way to the front of the group, sat on their knees, and waited. After a couple of minutes, they heard the teachers walk down the lane and onto the stage. Once on the stage the teachers began to assemble in a line in front of their students, and Ryuu noticed that one had an ice pack strapped to his head and a bandage around his nose. He averted his gaze.

He'll be feeling that in the morning, he thought, as he heard Aiolos give a small cough. He looked at his friend and shook his head slightly. He didn't want to aggravate the tense situation any further.

When all the teachers were assembled, there was a puff of smoke, and when it cleared, Ryuu's father stood before them in his grandmaster kimono. Jun briefly glanced at the teacher with the ice pack, but then returned his gaze to his students, and he smiled and spread his arms wide.

"Congratulations, all, on a job well done in tonight's final examination. Well done, well done indeed," he said.

When Jun lifted one of his arms, revealing an oriental box, Ryuu sucked in his breath. Beside him, he heard his teammates do the same. He watched as his father opened the lid, exposing small black-and-white medallions that bore the clan and school crest.

When the lid was completely open, Ryuu's father faced his students again.

"When I call your name, come forward and receive your master status. Allison Cromnae!"

Allison jumped to her feet, walked onto the stage, and smiled at Ryuu's father. Jun picked up a medallion and held it in front of her.

"Allison Cromnae, from this moment forward until forever, you shall be known as Red Bear because you're strong, fierce, and unstoppable until you achieve your goal." She bowed forward, and Jun slipped the medallion around her neck.

She bowed to him again and retook her seat.

"Erik Cromnae," the grandmaster said, and he picked up another medallion.

"Erik Cromnae, quick witted, cunning, strong, and yet with a kind heart. You shall be known as Silver Ape," he said.

Erik bowed, and Jun smiled. Then he slipped the medallion around Erik's neck. After another bow, Erik retook his position.

"Bryan Hunson," Jun called, and Bryan moved forward. The grandmaster picked up another medallion.

"A team player, a will of iron, loyal to a fault to your friends, to your family, to your cause, and to yourself. You shall be known as Iron Wolf," Ryuu's father said.

After more bowing, Bryan moved back to his friends.

"Aiolos Hudson." Aiolos quickly moved to the stage. Ryuu's father picked up another medallion and faced him.

"Quick witted, fast, reckless at times, boisterous, humorous, but with a will as free as the wind itself. You shall be known as White Flacon."

Ryuu's legs felt like lead as he anticipated his turn. Then his father looked in his direction and called out, "Dulglad Iga."

Ryuu frowned as Dulglad stepped forward, got his name and medallion, and retook his seat. One by one the other students went forward and received their names and medallions. After the last one walked back to retake his seat, Ryuu saw that there were no more medallions left for him.

He lowered his gaze. *I failed,* he thought. He seemed to feel Dulglad's nasty smile burning an imprint into his back, and a couple teachers chuckled.

Then Jun continued. "There is one student here whose name I didn't call yet. He tonight was forced into a test that called upon skills above and beyond the requirements of his graduation. He faced great peril that if he failed, which would have meant the loss of his own life. He has prospered in combat, evasion, gathering information, and cunning. He finished his mission, setting a new record for the course, and at the end he even helped his fallen foe.

"He is to be honored tonight for his impeccable bravery in the face of mortal danger and the unknown. So it's my great pleasure to call my son, Alec-Ryuu Jun Yamamoto," he said.

Ryuu looked up at his father and felt all eyes turn on him. After a moment, Allison gave him a small push, and he climbed to his feet. He walked onto the stage and stood before his father. His eyes darted to the teachers for a split second. Some looked unhappy, while others refused to meet his gaze.

His father smiled at him. Then, from his own neck, he unclasped his medallion and held it in his hands. "Alec-Ryuu Yamamoto, brave as a tiger, wise, cunning, kind at heart, righteous, comrade, a will of fire with a temper to match, and loyal to all who stand by you. You shall be known as Dragon's Fire, and it's my honor to make you, this day, Grandmaster," he said. He clasped the medallion around his son's neck.

Overcome with joy, Ryuu struggled to maintain his composure as he bowed to his father, who bowed back. Then he returned to his seat. He could barely contain his enthusiasm as his father addressed the assembled students.

"Again, well done to you all. It's been my deepest honor to have known and taught you. Whatever journey awaits you beyond the walls of this school, always remember the family that was forged here. And now, go forth, my brothers and sisters, and whatever path you choose, may you face it with your hearts open and your heads held high!"

As one, the students leapt to their feet, cheering.

Immediately, Ryuu was bombarded by his friends, who nearly tackled him to the ground.

"GRANDMASTER RYUU! HA! HA!" Bryan called out, shoving Ryuu's fist into the air.

"Positively spectacular!" Eric shouted, slapping Ryuu on the back.

"Everyone make way for Grandmaster Dragon's Fire!" declared Aiolos in a loud, formal voice.

Ryuu looked at everyone as he slipped off his mask. "Come on, guys, I'm not the only one who graduated tonight," he said, but inside, he wanted to jump for joy.

"Yeah, but none of us graduated as a grandmaster! Now, what are you made of? Make some noise!" Allison took his shoulders and shook him.

Ryuu finally gave in to his desires and jumped up and down, rejoicing as loudly as he could.

After almost an hour of celebrating, the students began to file out of the school and make their way home.

"I don't know about the rest of you, but I could eat a rhino," Eric said, as the group came out of the woods and Ryuu looked out at the rising sun.

"Come on; my house is closest," Ryuu said, leading the way.

The house was dark and quiet as they entered the kitchen. They moved silently, not wanting to wake his mother, and paused at the fridge. Before he could press the door release button to open the fridge, he paused. On the front of the unit, a light flashed. When Ryuu pressed it, a holographic note appeared.

Alec-Ryuu,
Went next door to help a neighbor. Be back soon. Pizza
in the fridge.
Mom
PS: Your father called and told me. I'm so proud of you.

"At least we get the place to ourselves," Aiolos said.

Ryuu looked at him. "Well, don't get any ideas. Your last one got me grounded for a month."

Despite his recent victory, he was still disappointed that no one had remembered his birthday. "I guess we've got pizza for my birth-day," he said gloomily. Then he pressed the release button, and the fridge door slid into itself.

As he took out the pizza, he heard his friends moan and groan behind him.

"Darn," Allison said. "That's today?"

"Not you guys, too!" he groaned, turning back to them.

"Oh, come on, Alec, give us a break," Bryan said regretfully running his hand down his face. "The finals drove it out of our minds," he finished and Ryuu looked over at him.

Not trusting himself to speak, Ryuu took a bite of cold pizza and turned to walk into the living room, sliding back the door. As he reached for the light button on the wall beside the door, the lights flicked themselves on.

At once, a strong sense of flight or fight bombarded Ryuu as he was instantly blinded and deafened by a variety of sights and sounds.

"SURPRISE!" the small crowd shouted.

Ryuu blinked at them, pizza dangling from his mouth.

An uncontrolled smile spread across his face as he read the signs on the walls. The first said, HAPPY BIRTHDAY! Below it, what looked like a hastily scrawled sign added, GRANDMASTER ALEC-RYUU JUN YAMAMATO!

"Oh, I hate you guys!" he barked. But he was laughing as his parents came over, and they formed a group hug.

"Happy birthday, my boy," his father said, slapping his shoulder.

"I can't believe you thought we would forget!" his mother said. "And you should have seen the look on your face when the light went on!" She gave him a peck on the cheek.

He tried not to think about his expression. Instead, he muttered, "Don't talk to me right now. I hate you!" His parents laughed along with him as friends and neighbors came forward to offer their birthday greetings.

THE DRAGON KNIGHTS

"Well, don't give us all the blame," his father said. "This wasn't completely our idea." Out of the corner of his eye, he saw his friends edging toward the back door.

The crowd parted a little, laughing, as Ryuu took off after his friends. As they barreled outside, he threw himself lengthwise, tackling them, and for a couple of minutes the friends wrestled across the ground, bits of grass and dust swirling in the air from their mock fight. Eventually they ended in a tangled heap. Catching his breath, looked back at the house, where the rest of the party guests were laughing and shaking their heads from the open door.

Ryuu quickly changed his clothes, and thirty minutes later they were all laughing, eating pizza, chips, and other party snacks, dancing, and playing games. The party lasted well through the day, although some of Ryuu's friends took quick naps to recover from the night's events. Through it all, despite his surprise at being successfully tricked, he couldn't help enjoying the double celebration.

As the sun began to set and the lights dimmed a little, his mother brought him a birthday cake with lit candles. The guests all sang "Happy Birthday," and Alec closed his eyes and made the same wish he made every year: to be reunited with his birth mother, wherever she was.

Smiling, he blew out the candles. The party guests applauded and brought forth gifts as his parents handed out the cake. He opened each present with eager hands and a glint in his eye. He was just admiring a new sky surfer when some of the guests parted to allow one of the oldest members of the community to come forward. Ryuu lowered his head in respect.

"Mr. Orleaus," he muttered.

Mr. Orleaus smiled at him. "Well, happy birthday, Mr. Yamamoto, and congratulations on becoming grandmaster." He bowed back.

Then a sneering voice from the doorway added, "Out of sheer dumb luck."

Ryuu and the others turned to see Dulglad, who was leaning

65

against a doorframe. He was surrounded by his friends, who all wore the same hard looks on their faces.

"Oh, is that what your own father said?" Ryuu asked. He heard a couple of his friend's snicker.

Dulglad's face hardened at once. Mr. Orleaus ignored the tension and continued.

"The gift that I bring to you this special day is not like one you've received yet, for it's a story. A story that's a part of us, of a time that's long since been over. A time when we didn't have to hide on backwater planets. A time when fear didn't run our lives, and we lived in peace and harmony in the age of technology of Humans, of magic, and of Dragons. The age of the Dragon Knights."

A couple people looked at each other muttering.

"And you would condemn us by telling this story? You stupid old man!" Dulglad snapped. He stalked forward, and Ryuu stepped in his way.

He and Dulglad stared daggers at each other. Finally, Ryuu broke the silence and said, "It's my birthday, and a gift to me. I'll hear it. Anyone who doesn't want to hear it and prefers to forget our past, when we lived in peace, may leave."

Then he added, "Besides, you forget that we're already condemned. If the Black Dragon's forces ever find us, we will all be captured and sold as slaves. Or annihilated."

He glanced at the people around him. Some were muttering, but no one moved to leave. Ryuu looked back at Dulglad and his friends. "And you?" he asked.

One by one, Dulglad and his friends stepped back, but they didn't leave. Ryuu, struggling to keep his breathing calm, finally returned his attention to Mr. Orleaus. Their eyes locked for a moment, and Ryuu motioned for the man to continue.

Mr. Orleaus bowed again, moving to the center of the living room. Then he cleared his throat and turned to face them, arms wide.

"Listen well, for the tale I tell is a part of everyone in this room.

We are each controlled by our past, and unless we learn from it, we have no chance of a better future.

"Ages upon ages ago, after centuries of hiding, people and creatures of magic revealed themselves to the non-magical beings. For a long period after that, they worked happily together and reached for the stars. They even found and restored dead planets, including the one we now stand on.

"Unfortunately, prejudice and mistrust began to grow between the magical and the non-magical races. One day the tension rose so high, both parties seemed to snap. No one knows who started the fighting, but it grew to such an intensity that both sides realized that if they continued, they would annihilate each other.

"Therefore, one-day emissaries from both sides called for a cease-fire. For an uncounted time, they negotiated, until they finally decided to find a way to link the races, binding their fates together as one, for the sake of peace for all. Ultimately, so that conflict could never rise between the nations again, they decided to create a band of immortal warriors to keep the peace and bring justice to the stars.

"These warriors would not be a part of one of the nations, but both. This would ensure that no warrior would ever be biased to other party. Rather, they would honor and respect a perfect blend of magic and technology. Through this agreement, the emissaries planted the seeds that founded one of the greatest and bravest groups of men and women in all the ages: The Dragon Knights.

"For years, the non-magical beings pooled all their knowledge of technology together, a knowledge that surpasses ours even today. Then seven members of the most powerful magical race, the Dragons, poured their magic into that greatest technology, and thus they forged the armors of the Dragon Knights.

"With the armors completed, the Dragon Knights chartered a star ship dubbed the *Sherwood* to reach out to all the people of the stars. And for millenniums, peace reigned throughout the nations, and under the protection of the Dragon Knights, all people and creatures flourished."

Mr. Orleaus paused and shook his head sadly. He said, "If only it could have lasted."

Then he sighed deeply and continued. "From within the ranks of the Magical and Non-Magical Council whose members included the representatives of all races, a mighty Black Dragon considered the pact between the magical and the non-magical to be a joke. His objections grew to such an extent that one of the leaders of the council, the Gold Dragon, who was the strongest of all the magical beings, forced him to leave. For a few more years, peace continued, and the Black Dragon's words were forgotten.

"Then one day, on an agricultural planet, a shadow fell as the Black Dragon and his army descended upon the people, enslaving the non-magical beings. At first, the Gold Dragon sent emissaries to the Black Dragon, but all messages were ignored, and many messengers were killed. Soon the Black Dragon's forces had spread like an evil wave. Then the cold day came when war was declared, and the Knights were called in to lead the forces of the nations.

"As powerful as the armies and navies were, they were no match against the power of the Black Dragon. The only one who could match his might was the Gold Dragon, and when the two finally met in combat, a battle waged like never before. The lives of all free people hung in the balance.

"For days, the two dragons battled for supremacy over the other. When the battle finally settled, the Gold Dragon was slain, and the Black Dragon proclaimed himself ruler over all. Over the years, hope faded as one by one the Knights were hunted down and killed, their armors seized.

"And from the day of the last Dragon Knight's death and the disappearance of the Sherwood nearly a century ago, enslavement and fear have met the masses of the people of both nations, forcing ours into hiding. No one knows what happened to the Sherwood, and the only clue to its location was a message transmitted from the last Knight, saying that it is 'within the eye of the god of the gods.' But from these ashes was born the Resistance, whose leader is shrouded in shadow and mystery. Now fighters both magical and non-magical gather to await the next generation of Dragon Knights, and with them the birth of the next Gold Dragon," Mr. Orleaus concluded.

The room was silent as the story ended. Some people exchanged uneasy looks, and Ryuu saw his father put a comforting hand on his mother's shoulder. After a couple minutes, people started muttering. Taking a breath, Ryuu wiped his eye and looked out at the setting sun.

Clearing his throat, he thanked Mr. Orleaus, picked up a drink, and walked to the middle of the room. When he was sure he had everyone's attention, he said, "Well, I just want to thank everyone for this party, though some of you whom I won't name are now on my hit list." A couple people laughed, and he smiled at his friends. Then he continued, "But again, thank you for coming, even if it's for someone as boring as me . . ."

A few more people laughed, while others just shook their head.

". . . and for all the gifts and everything. I know it's starting to get late, so I'll conclude with this." He raised his drink.

"To the return of the Knights!" he declared.

Around him, people froze in their tracks and stared. For a long moment, he stood there with a raised drink as only silence met him. Then Bryan, Allison, Erik, and Aiolos raised their drinks.

Bryan said, "To the return of the Knights!"

"Dragon Knights unite!" Allison offered.

"To the Knights!" Erik chimed in. "And the downfall of the Black Dragon!"

"Dragon Knights kick butt!"

Everyone looked at Aiolos for a second. Then all of the guests raised their drinks, and soon the room was filled with a milder version of that toast. And, as Ryuu smiled, they all drank.

CHAPTER 8

THE RIGHT THINKING

A S ALEC WAS in this kitchen saying goodbye to a few of his neighbors, his friends came up, and Allison slapped him on his shoulder.

"Now you definitely remind me of me, because the speech was nice and short, and that toast took a lot of guts!" she said and handed him another drink.

"Thanks." He smiled. "You guys do realize that I'm going to get you back for this, right?"

Aiolos said, "Oh come on, man, you know you loved it."

Ryuu laughed in spite of himself and nodded. Then, as they moved back toward the living room, he froze. He could hear Dulglad's loud voice coming from outside.

"That freak is going to get us all killed one day!"

Ryuu's face hardened, and his friends frowned. When Ryuu glanced out the window, he saw Dulglad talking to his friends.

"If we've got to deal with a son like this, I can only imagine what kind of person his mother was," he heard Melinda say.

"Probably some drifter colony bum or drunk," Kade said.

Ryuu clenched his fingers and started to shake with rage.

"More likely she was a lowly slave girl," Dulglad said.

The glass in Ryuu's hand shattered under his grip.

Before his friends could stop him, he raced out the door and, launching himself from the porch, nailed Dulglad with a flying sidekick. Duglad lurched forward as Ryuu landed nimbly on his feet. For a second, Dulglad's friends looked at Ryuu, dumbfounded. Then Bamber and Melinda took out small rods that extended to bo-staffs, and came at him.

Kade started with a punch, which Ryuu countered with a kick to his chest, sending him back before he side-kicked Babieca to his right. He turned in time to grab Melinda's arm and threw her over his shoulder as she attacked with her staff. As he slipped her staff from her grasp, he ducked under a swing from Bamber.

As Ryuu turned to face Bamber, he kicked Kade back to the ground and blocked another attack from Bamber's staff. When Bamber withdrew his staff, Ryuu dropped down and swept his legs out from under him. After blocking a blow from Melinda with the staff, he then jumped to his feet, locked her arm up, and threw her to the ground.

Releasing the staff, he then did a couple handsprings, landing back on his feet. Babieca and Kade grabbed his arms as Bamber came at him, fist raised. He leapt up and wrapped his ankles around Bamber's neck, and using his body weight, he went to the ground and sent Bamber over him onto his back behind him. Leaping to his feet, he side-kicked Kade back to the ground, ducked under a crescent kick from Babieca, and, standing, backhanded him across the face.

When none of them got up, Ryuu walked over to Dulglad, and the two faced off. Dulglad threw a crescent kick, which Ryuu ducked under, and tried to follow up with a spin kick, which Ryuu blocked. Then Ryuu counter-punched him in the face, sending him spinning. Stunned by the blow, Dulglad froze as Ryuu leapt up, nailing him across the face with a spin kick that sent him to the ground.

His anger still boiling, Ryuu reached down and dragged Dulglad to his feet, holding him by his collar. Then he turned Dulglad to face him.

"*Call my mother a lowly slave, will you?*" he demanded. He threw his opponent ten feet, where he landed hard on the roof of a hover car.

With one leap, Ryuu was on the hood, crouching over him. This time he grabbed Dulglad by the neck, fist pulled back to strike.

"RYUU!"

He froze and looked back. His friends were staring at him from the bottom of the steps.

"Ryuu, he may have it coming, but he's not worth it!" Bryan said.

Ryuu glanced down at Dulglad, who cowered beneath him.

Allison yelled, "Ryuu, we heard what he said—a lot of people did—and believe me, I'd do worse and you know it. But you have to ask yourself, would hitting him make you any different?"

"My sister's right, Ryuu," Erik insisted. "The taste won't be sweet but bitter."

"Do the right thing and make both of your mothers proud," Aiolos said. "Be the bigger man and let him go."

Ryuu remained still, breathing hard, trying to get his inflamed temper in check. Then, with a brief yell, he shot his fist forward and struck the force field next to Dulglad's head. Slowly he let Dulglad go, stood, and hopped back down from the car.

"You're right," he muttered. He started to walk toward his friends.

"Coward!" Dulglad yelled from behind him.

"Hey!" Allison shouted. "He kicked all your asses! More important, by walking away he just proved he's more of a man than you'll ever be! So why don't you shut up!"

"Besides," Ryuu growled, "I still owe you one." As everyone looked at him, he spun around and threw a hard punch into Dulglad's face, launching the teen off his feet.

"That's for the flash bang and for nearly getting me killed!" he snapped, jabbing a finger.

Dulglad clutched his broken nose while people gawked.

There was a soft cough from the porch, and when they all turned toward the sound, Ryuu saw his parents. They were standing on the porch with their arms crossed. Jun held Ryuu's gaze for several long moments before they slowly turned and went inside.

"Oh, man," Ryuu muttered.

Aiolos patted his back. "If you survive, we'll see you later."

Ryuu managed a weak smile and nodded.

"I'll see you tomorrow, guys," he muttered. Then he took a final look at Dulglad and his friends. Bamba and Kade were still moaning on the ground, while Babieca was clearly nursing an injury. Turning his back, he went inside.

The living room was dimly lit, but most of the plates and glasses had already been cleared away. Sitting on their knees in the middle of the room were his parents, eyes closed.

Sighing, Ryuu started toward his room. Then his mother's voice called out, "Ryuu, come back in and sit by us."

Sighing again, he rubbed the back of his neck and stopped. Then he gave a quick moan and said, "It's still my birthday. Can't this wait?"

"Birthday or no birthday, you'll listen now," his father said firmly.

Ryuu remained still for a moment. Then slowly, face downcast, he walked forward and slipped down to his knees before them. When he was seated, they opened their eyes and looked at him. For a few seconds he held each of their gazes in turn. Then he lowered his eyes to the floor.

"Tell us the most important thing we taught you," his father said.

Ryuu shifted his weight from side to side. "To possess the right frame of mind in order to gain strength, knowledge, and peace."

For a second, the room was filled with silence. Then his mother placed her hands lovingly on his cheeks and said, "Alec-Ryuu, we've tried so hard to channel your anger about the fact that your birth mother had to leave you. But so much is left. You've chosen to face it alone, but you must not forget your friends. And you must not forget us."

Then she cupped his chin and lifted his head so his gaze met her eyes. He looked at her, breathing in gasps, and a tear formed in the corner of his eye. Before it could fall, his mother pulled him into an embrace, and he cried into her. Soon his father's strong arms held them both tightly as Ryuu cried in wheezing gasps.

"Shhh," his mother soothed him. "We'll always be here, Ryuu. We always will." She rubbed his back.

"Why . . . why . . . why did she leave me?" he said, between gasps.

His parents looked at him and then at each other. After a few moments, his father said, "Because she loved you so much that she would rather have died than to see you come to harm."

His mother took his hand in her own. "Either one of us would do the same for you now."

Ryuu knew she was speaking the truth.

CHAPTER 9
THE NEXT GENERATION

THAT NIGHT RYUU lay on his mat, his thoughts on his birth mother. He still stung with the shame of the fight with Dulglad, but more than that, he couldn't stop going over what his parents had said.

Did they know her? he asked himself repeatedly. *Why did she bring me here?*

Finally, a clock in the hall chimed midnight, and he rolled over and went to sleep.

About an hour later, he awoke with a jerk as he ears filled with a loud ringing sound. Twisting around, he used his feet to turn his clock to check the time. He growled when he saw it was only one in the morning.

Still moaning, he slammed himself back down and stuffed his head under his pillow. For half an hour, he tossed and turned, trying to get rid of the sound.

Finally, he gave up. As he got to his feet, he growled, "Whoever is making that noise had better find themselves a tombstone!"

He continued to block his ears as he searched the house for the cause of the noise. Ten minutes later, he silently crept to his parent's room. He froze when he looked in; they were sleeping as if nothing was happening. To him, however, the sound was so painful he began to grit his teeth.

Leaving his parents to undisturbed, he turned and quietly walked into the bathroom. As he crossed the threshold, the lights turned on. He stepped in front of the mirror, and a little holographic woman appeared on the counter.

"Good evening, Ryuu. Please state requirement."

"Medical," he muttered. From the ceiling a ring descended and ran down him.

"Bio temperature: normal. Digestive tract: normal. Skeletal: normal. Brain activity: normal. Abrasions: negative—"

"Primary focus, ear canal, left and right, intense ringing sound," he said through clenched teeth, and the ring raised itself to hover around his head level.

The computer was silent for a moment. Then, "Ear canals: normal; cause of ringing sound: unknown. Do you still require assistance?"

"No," Ryuu moaned. He moved out of the bathroom before the computer would call him crazy.

Back out in the hall, his hands clamped around his ears, he slowly made his way to the front door and slipped outside to the porch. Taking a couple steps forward, he moaned again. It seemed like the noise was even louder outside of the house. After taking a couple steps forward, he stumbled down the stairs and landed hard on his back.

He quickly rolled onto his elbows, hands flying to his ears. When he looked up, he was surprised to see his friends walking down the street toward him, hands over their ears.

"You all right?" Allison yelled when they reached him. He got to his feet.

"Yeah, mostly!" he shouted back. "You hear it too?" he shouted at Bryan when he got close.

"What?" he barked back. For a second, Bryan uncovered his ear. Then he snapped his hand back in place.

Almost doubled over, Aiolos stumbled a bit as he stepped forward, ears covered. "Whoever is making this noise had better have a death wish, because I'm going to kill him," he shouted.

"What?" the others yelled.

Ryuu waved his head left and right. "It's coming from that way!" He tilted his head and nodded toward the forest.

"What?" his friends demanded.

He sighed, removed his hand from his right ear, and pointed. As soon as he did, the group moved in that direction. Moments later, they were walking out of the village and into the forest. Deaf to the world around them, they stumbled through the forest. Erik emerged first, but as he did so, he nearly fell into the ravine they raced through and jumped over during the exam.

Ryuu and Allison darted forward and grabbed him as he flailed his arms for balance. For what seemed like an hour, the three teetered along the edge before they were able to pull him back to solid ground. Breathing hard, Ryuu clamped his hands over his sore ears as Erik grasped his sister in a tight bear hug. Ryuu looked around as the others came out of the forest, and Allison gently pushed Erik away before he smothered her.

Ryuu looked over the edge and cursed silently. The sound was coming from down the ravine, but he could see no way down. As he turned to shout this information to his friends, he eyed a cliff that ran to one side. Narrowing his eyes, he examined it more closely, and after a moment, gritting his teeth in pain, he picked up a stone from the ground and tossed it.

He watched the stone disappear over a dip and then reappear on another ledge. Excited, he stepped closer, looked down, and saw that a series of rocks jutted from the side of the cliff and ran down it. Smiling, he turned and saw the others hip deep in a silent debate.

He tried to signal them. When that failed, he flicked his foot and sent a pebble flying in their direction. He cringed when it struck Aiolos on the side of his head.

Aiolos gave a yelp and faced Ryuu, who, after a moment, bobbed his head in the direction of what he had found. They came over, Aiolos nursing the spot where he had been hit, and looked down. They turned and some gave him the thumbs up and waved for him to go first.

He nodded, stepped in front of them, and, taking a deep breath, took the first step on to what appeared to be thin air but was actually the first rock in the series of steps leading to the bottom of the ravine. For ten minutes, they walked down the cliff, and as they did, Ryuu was able to lower his hands. The volume of the ringing sound descended as they did. When they finally came to the end, they all stood on a lone cliff edge in the middle of the ravine.

"Well, at least it's quieter down here," Bryan said.

Ryuu looked around. There, shadowing them all, was a cave set into the wall of the ravine.

After a moment, Aiolos waved his hand and mouthed, "After you."

Sighing, Ryuu walked into the gloom. Inside, he blinked a couple of times to get his eyes used to the darkness. Then the others joined him.

"So, did anyone here bring a flashlight?" Aiolos asked.

"You'd think after all these centuries, they'd come up with a better name," Erik said.

"Erik, I didn't ask for a linguistics discussion; I just want to know if anyone brought one."

"Nope."

"Didn't think I'd need one."

"Negative."

"I was concentrating on saving my hearing."

"Never seem to need one."

Aiolos scowled and turned to Ryuu. "Well, Mr. Owl Eyes, lead the way!"

They laughed as they walked through the cave. Ryuu guided them as best he could, but every now and then, they still either stumbled or bumped their heads. After several more minutes, Aiolos let out a large groan and rubbed his scalp.

"Okay, that's it. If I get hit in the head one more time—"

"What are you going to do, Aiolos, scream like a girl?" Allison asked.

"No, that would be your department, considering you're a girl."

"I'll show you what kind of a girl I am!"

Ryuu turned in time to see Allison pounce in Aiolos's direction, but he dodged out of the way, so instead she attacked Bryan. Ryuu rolled his eyes as Bryan tried to fend her off.

"Allison, let Bryan go. Aiolos is at your nine o'clock," he said.

Allison, who just put Bryan into a chokehold, froze.

"Oh, thanks a lot, man," Aiolos muttered, and Allison whipped her head around to his direction.

Smiling, Ryuu turned to continue to examine the area. The noise just an annoying low buzz to him now. He'd barely turned his head when he froze.

"Allison, let him go," he said, narrowing his eyes to look more closely at what he was seeing.

"Not a chance. I'm not done yet," she said. She still held Aiolos in her grasp, even though he kept moaning "Uncle" over and over.

In one motion, Ryuu pulled them apart and held them up so their feet were dangling.

"I said, ENOUGH! I think we're here!" he snapped. The others turned toward him, and Allison stopped fighting to free herself.

"What makes you say that?" Eric asked.

Ryuu put his friends down and walked over to two stalagmites on a flat-topped rock. On the rock, which was about waist high, was a gold-embroidered, wooden box.

What the hell is this doing in here? he thought as he opened the lid.

An instant later, he jumped back, his hands flying up to shield his eyes from the sudden burst of multicolored light that radiated out of the box. The others also shielded their eyes, but they recovered more quickly as Ryuu stumbled about, blinded. Before he could hit the wall headfirst, Allison and Bryan grabbed him and held him back.

"Keep your eyes closed. Then slowly open them," Allison said, beside him.

He followed her directions, blinked a couple of times, and stood straight.

"I hate it when that happens," he muttered, turning to face the others. "Still want my Owl Eyes, Aiolos?"

Aiolos shrugged. Then they all turned their focus back to the box.

Now the cave was filled with the iridescent light from the box, and they could see clearly. The box contained seven bracelets, each imbedded with a crystal that glowed a different color.

"What the hell are those?" Erik asked.

"I have no idea," Ryuu said slowly. He raised a hand to reach in.

At once, the light from the crystals began to pulse, and the bracelets rose from the box. Stepping back, Ryuu and the other watched in awe as they rose into the air to hover near the ceiling of the cave. As the seconds crept by, the pulsing light increased until it seemed consistent. Then, without warning, all but three of the bracelets shot at them and wrapped themselves around the friends' wrists.

Ryuu and the others yelped in surprise and jumped back. Ryuu then closed his eyes as the light became blinding again. Twisting his arm to keep the light out of his eyes, he clutched his wrist and raised it above his head.

A booming voice declared in his mind, "AS *FORETOLD BY*

ANCIENTS PAST! SO SHALL ARISE THE NEXT GENERATION OF DRAGON KNIGHTS!"

Mercifully, the light dimmed and went out. Ryuu opened his eyes to see the cave dark once more. Breathing hard, he blinked a couple times to get used to the dark. Then he looked at the bracelet on his wrist. When he glanced up again, he saw that the last three bands had disappeared.

Slowly, his turned toward his friends.

"Everyone okay?" he asked, and they each gave an affirmative.

"Did anyone else hear that?" Bryan asked. "As foretold . . ."

". . . by ancients past . . ." Aiolos continued.

". . . so shall arise . . ." Erik said.

". . . the next generation…" Allison added.

". . . of Dragon Knights."

As Ryuu finished, the cave rang with silence.

On a distant planet.

Elaine's eyes shot open and she raised her head, and slipping from the covers of her bed, went to the window and looked up at one of the stars. "It has begun," she muttered, shifting some hair from her face.

On another planet

Another eye opened that was fiery red surrounded by darkness. "So," a voice said in a growling tone. "A new generation has taken up the mantle."

CHAPTER 10

THE ANUBIS AND THE DARK ELF

RYUU WAS SO tired, he hardly remembered stumbling back home, although he did recall that the friends had speculated in great length about the potential recipients of the other three bracelets. Did they live in neighboring villages on other planets? When would they all meet? And did the Black Dragon know about this? How much danger were they now in?

He slipped into his room just as the sun was coming up. Giving a big yawn, he made for his bed with all the intention of a nice long sleep.

He was just pulling back the blankets when he heard his mother's voice.

"Alec-Ryuu, is that you?"

Ryuu gave a small moan. "Just making the bed," he mumbled as his door opened.

"Well, breakfast will be ready in a few minutes," she said. She gave him a brief smile and then left.

He looked longingly at his bed and then turned, went to his dresser, and pulled out some clothes. When he was dressed, he walked down to the kitchen and sat at the table beside his father, who was already drinking his tea and reading the holo-paper. Behind him, Chikako was just taking breakfast off the stove.

Hearing Ryuu come in, his father looked up and smiled.

"Some party yesterday," he said. The holographic paper vanished, and he placed the emitter pad aside.

"You're not kidding," Ryuu, said. He stifled a huge yawn as his mother put his breakfast in front of him as both eyed him. "Didn't get much sleep last night," he explained, and his parents nodded.

"Must have been the cake; too much sugar or something," his mother said.

"Yeah, maybe," Ryuu said. He took a bite of French toast. As usual, it spoke to Chikako's skill in the kitchen. it was delicious.

The rest of the meal began as normal, with the three joking and talking. As it progressed, Ryuu noticed that his parents kept shooting glances at him, yet every time he felt their eyes on him, they quickly looked away, and conversation went on.

When his plate was empty, Ryuu stood and began to carry it to the counter.

"We'll take care of it, Alec-Ryuu. You go and meet your friends," his mother said. She reached for the plate.

"Okay, see you guys later," he said. He grabbed his sky surfer and bolted toward the door.

On his way out, he saw his father place his elbows on the table, interlace his fingers, and rest his chin on them.

"Too much sugar . . . hmmm." These were the last words he heard his father say as he closed the door behind him.

❋

Not long after, Ryuu lay on his hovering sky surfer near the stone archway and crystal. He'd nodded off a little while ago and was still half asleep. For almost an hour, he remained in that position, catching up on his rest and listening to the sounds around him.

"I had a feeling you guys would be coming here," he said suddenly. He opened his eyes and looked at his friends.

"How do you do that?" Allison demanded. The others' expressions posed similar questions as they collapsed their sky surfers and faced him.

Soon they were all sitting in silence, simply starting at each other.

"So, are we going to talk about what happened last night?" Aiolos finally asked. He pulled back his sleeve and revealed his bracelet, which had a clear white crystal.

"I still don't know what happened to begin with," Ryuu said. He looked at his own bracelet, which bore a ruby-red crystal.

"What did the voice mean by 'Next Generation of Dragon Knights'?" Erik asked. He rubbed his own bracelet, which had a blue crystal.

"Not quite sure." Bryan looked down at his deep-green crystal. "And what do these have to do with the knights?"

After giving his bracelet a very close look, Ryuu paused, taking it in. There seemed to be weapons engraved on the sides.

"You know . . . maybe, just maybe . . ."

A second later, Allison smirked and said, "You gotta be kidding me! You think these are the legendary armors of the Dragon Knights?" Her violet crystal seemed to flash in the sunlight.

Ryuu shrugged and said, "Well, what else could they be?"

She rolled her eyes. "If these bracelets were the only armor of the original Dragon Knights, they must have won their battles by sending their enemies into fatal peals of laughter," she said.

"But remember what Mr. Orleaus said," Ryuu persisted. "The original Dragon Knights were a blend of advanced technology and magic."

"Ryuu, it's not possible," Erik said gently. "It takes six bands to make our hockey armor—"

But before he could finish his sentence, the crystals on their bracelets began to pulse.

❊

Inside the cave by the cliff, Ryuu's father, with a grim expression on this face, followed the beam of his flashlight. Eventually, the beam fell on the open lid of the box, and he paused. For a moment, he stood in shocked silence. Then, slowly, he drew closer and stared down at the empty box.

"And so it begins . . ." Jun muttered. "I just pray you're ready, Ryuu."

He turned to leave. "Spirits above and below, please be ready."

Jun headed home in a daze, ignoring the folks who called out to him in greeting and missing their startled expressions when he didn't respond. Inside, he found Chikako where he'd left her at the kitchen table, a cup of untouched tea before her.

"It happened, didn't it?" she asked.

All he could do was nod.

Her eyes closed. "Do you think he's ready?" she asked finally, looking at him.

With a sigh, he sat beside her. "We taught him well . . ." He took her hand in both of his. "But it's out of our hands now."

For a few seconds, there was nothing but silence between them. Then he said, "I think it's time to tell him."

❊

As Ryuu looked down at the pulsing crystal on this bracelet, the alarms at the village began blaring.

"The planetary sensors must have been triggered!" he barked, and they leapt to their feet.

Another sound caused him to look up. Spinning around, he

watched, open mouthed, as four bright, flame-red specks streaked across the sky.

He followed their progress closely as they flew over the village. Then he caught his breath. The streaks had altered course and were coming around.

"Scouts or slavers; they're heading toward the village," Ryuu shouted.

He grabbed his sky surfer, and his friends followed quickly behind as he headed into the forest to keep out of sight and observe what was unfolding. As he raced along, he watched the sky. When he stopped at the edge of the woods, a transport ship and several fighter ships descended from the balls of fire and moved directly toward the village.

The transport was a little bigger than a large house. Its wide forward section was almost oval in shape, with sharp, angular edges. At the rear, a tail jutted out, thinning with a pair of short wings at the end. The cockpit had laser cannons on rotating torrents and missile tubes on either side of it, as well as a larger torrent on top and bottom.

Each fighter was the size of a hover car, with the main body almost circular in shape and two wings attached to the sides that jutted forward and slightly back. There were also lasers between the wings and missile tubes embedded within them.

Ryuu felt a chill creep down his spine. The front of each vessel included the design of a dragon skull.

"The Black Dragon," he muttered.

They watched as the ships lowered their landing skids and touched down just outside the village.

"We've got to do something!" Bryan yelled.

"I say we kick butt," Allison said. She snapped her fist into her hand.

"And how do you plan to do that? Throw rocks at them?" Erik moved to hold her back as the ramp of the transport lowered.

When the door opened, twenty robotic Sentinels disembarked. They looked like muscular men, but they were a little taller than average-sized men, and they stood on raised heels of clawed feet. Their metal armor was smooth, with various slots around their arms and thighs. There were gears on the side of the arms as well as a line of blades.

Ryuu's attention was immediately drawn to their heads, for they weren't shaped like human, elf, or any dark creature. Instead, each head was formed like the head of a two-horned dragon with red eyes.

Ryuu and his friends watched as the Sentinels moved into formation beside the ship and began to march into the village. Then a chill moved through him again as another figure came down the ramp and started moving toward the forest. It was as tall as a man, with skin as black as night over toned, hard muscles, clawed hands, and clawed feet. A gold cape whipped in the wind behind the figure, and gold bands and manacles decorated its arms. Black hair so thick it seemed a solid mass ran along the back of its head, which was in the shape of a wolf or a jackal.

Next to it walked a woman wearing black and blood-red clothes. She had long white hair that reached down to her hips. Poking out of her hair were the pointed ears of an elf. As her head turned and Ryuu saw a glimpse of her face from afar, and he realized that her skin was deep purple, and her white eyes had a ridge in the shape of a crescent moon between them.

"An Anubis and a Dark Elf," Ryuu said under his breath.

He took cover behind a cluster of trees, and his friends joined him.

"If they have an Anubis and a Dark Elf with them, then they must not plan to take any prisoners," Erik muttered.

"Or very few. But how'd they find us with the new dampening system? The last group we had to fend off was years ago, and we made sure they didn't transmit anything," Bryan muttered.

Ryuu's eyes slowly shifted to the bracelet on his wrist. Then his eyes shot back as the Anubis turned toward the village and began to speak in a deep, growling voice.

"I'm Maltanore," he declared. "We know you're here. We detected you from orbit two days ago. Come out now and surrender. If you cooperate, we will spare your lives and sell you as slaves."

Ryuu felt his face harden. He looked at his friends. Now they had their answer.

Before he could move, citizens came out of hiding places in the village below. Shooting blasters and defenses and started firing at the Sentinels. As one, the Sentinels each raised an arm. A slot on each arm raised up revealing a blaster cannon, and the Sentinels returned fire as they charged into the village.

The friends watched from afar as people fell under a barrage of laser fire.

"WELL, WE'VE GOT TO DO SOMETHING!" Ryuu yelled. Then, as he and his friends moved toward the village, the crystal on his wristband began to pulse again.

Ryuu's father dragged a wounded man behind an overturned hover car. Blood leaked from a wound in the man's shoulder, and Jun ripped some of his own clothes to make a bandage.

"You're going to be just fine," he told the man.

He turned at the sound of heavy feet and saw a Sentinel move to face them. As it slowly raised its cannon, there was a flash of movement across its neck, from shoulder to hip and across the waist. The Sentinel was still for a moment. Then those sections fell to the ground, revealing Chikako, a laser-edged Kanata in both her hands.

"Now don't go all to pieces on me," she said, rushing over to take the bandage and apply it to the man's wound.

Jun fired a few rounds over the top of the car.

"They're winning, aren't they?" the man demanded.

"What do you think?" an eerie voice answered from behind them.

Jun looked up to see the Dark Elf hovering over them. When she slowly raised her hand, a ball of swirling black energy appeared in her palm.

Jun tackled Chikako out of the way. As he covered her, he felt the heat wave of an explosion. Something hard hit the ground in front of them.

Uncovering his head, Jun looked around. The man's disemboweled torso lay on the ground before him, his blank, empty eyes staring at the sky.

As Jun reached for Chikako's hand, a pair of clawed feet stepped into view. He looked up into the face of Maltanore, who was flanked by a pair of Sentinels.

"Mortals," the Anubis muttered, and Jun felt gripped by a wave of fear.

To his surprise, Maltanore's attention suddenly turned toward the sky. Following his gaze, Jun saw five objects streak down from the sky in an arrow formation. Pulling up, they flew into the village, and as they drew near it, Jun saw that it appeared to be several young people on sky surfers.

As the leader neared a passing Sentinel, he drew back a fist, and as he passed, he punched a big chunk from the Sentinel, causing it to twist from the blow. Sparks flew everywhere as it fell to the ground.

Jun and Chikako joined a small crowd of people who had gathered to watch the flyers. Overhead, two of the flyers rolled, which caused them to drop to the ground. After flipping in midair, they each landed on bended knee. Then they stood up as the remaining flyers hovered above.

In appearance, they looked like well-muscled humans. They each had separated armored plates along the major muscle groups; these plates were surrounded by a black material that moved smoothly as the figures moved. Low on the hips was a pair of metallic rods with the same black material making up the grip. With emitters on both sides of the rods.

However, there were differences between them. One in particular had the slim but powerful build of a young woman. The main feature that Jun noticed was their helmets and masks.

All of them were the shape of a dragon's head. The male on the ground had a round blunt snout with a small ridge between the eyes. On both corners of his head he had a slightly swept-back horn, with a third in the middle of the head.

The female, who was one of the two figures on the ground, had a more pointed snout. She had a single sweptback horn in the middle of the top of her head. On the side of her head, she had long, large, pointed sweptback ears.

One of the flyers who was still in the air had a head with an elongated wolfish snout dragon face. With catfish-like whiskers that weaved through the air as if they were being billowed in a strong wind. Two swept back horns were set in the corners of his head.

The fourth—and most muscled—of the group had a slightly wider and squat face than the rest, with a thick, shallow dome in the center of the forehead and a line of spikes running along the side of the head.

The last one had two front and back sweeping frills on either side of its head; and two horns swept back over his head.

"It can't be . . ." Maltanore gaped.

"Oh, it is," the male figure on the ground said.

"Dragon Knights," Jun said in wonder.

Maltanore roared, "SENTINELS ATTACK! KILL EVERYONE! FIGHTERS INTO THE AIR! BOMBARD THE VILLAGE!"

At once, several Sentinels turned and raised their arms to fire at the Dragon Knights. In a flash of movement, the two knights on the ground charged forward. In a shower of sparks, the male forced the arm of the nearest Sentinel back as the cannon fired, blowing its own head off.

Beside him, the female Dragon Knight ripped off the arm of a Sentinel and then used the arm to knock off its head.

The other fighters started to lift off, and the male Dragon Knight pointed as he yelled, "Get them!" in an altered voice.

At once, two of the Knights in the air rocketed up after the fighters, while the one with the largest muscles dropped down to join the fight on the group. The leaner male nailed a Sentinel with a spin kick, knocking its head off the jaw spinning away, but when he turned, Maltanore nailed him with a hard uppercut to the chest, launching him off his feet.

"Ryuu...," Jun muttered in fear and worry as he watched him soar over the village by the blow with Maltanore leaping after him. As he glanced at the Knights both on the ground and in the sky he had a pretty good idea who was in the armors.

In the air, Aiolos weaved on his board, dodging laser fire from the fighter who was hot on his tail.

"This would be so much easier if I could shoot back!" he snapped, rolling to dodge more lasers. For a brief second, he shifted his attention to the fighter holo sensor and armor readouts in front of his face.

Suddenly a message flashed across the screen.

"Interface commencing?" he muttered, and at a sound, he looked down.

Below him, thin wires extended from the armor of his thigh and connected to his sky surfer. At once, his surfer began to change. Short, trapezoid wings with lasers embedded inside emerged from the base. Behind him, the engine grew slightly larger, and a set of missile tubes appeared underneath on either side of an intake ramp.

"Now this I like," he said with a grin.

After glancing over his shoulder, he pulled his board into a sharp turn, firing the lasers at the fighter as it passed, blowing off a section over the missiles. Righting the board behind the fighter, he rocketed after it, and a targeting scanner appeared.

"See how you like it! FIRE MISSILES!" he yelled, and his missiles launched forward and slammed into the exposed missiles, detonating them and blowing the wing off.

"OH, YEAH! WHO'S THE MAN?" Aiolos shouted. He thrust his hands into the air in triumph as the fighter dropped from the sky, spinning like a top.

❉

Ryuu tumbled over the village and came down in the forest, snapping branches as he went until he hit the ground. As he came to a skidding and rolling stop, he moaned and pushed himself onto one knee. Around him was a great clatter of wildlife as the forest animals rushed to flee the scene.

"Ow," he muttered. He clutched his armored chest while the torso section of his holo armor read out flashed.

He looked up just as Maltanore landed in front of him on crouched legs.

"So you're the next generation of Dragon Knights," he said as Ryuu climbed to his feet. "What makes you think you'll have any success where others have failed?"

Before Ryuu could reply, the sounds of an explosion filled the air above them. Looking up, Ryuu saw one of the fighters lose a wing and fall, spinning to the ground out of sight as the blast of the crash reverberated through the air.

"Looks to me like we're doing just fine," Ryuu said.

Maltanore chuckled and whipped off his cape. Now he was

dressed only in a cloth, which was wrapped around his waist and his jewelry.

"A few Sentinels and fighters are easily replaced," the Anubis said. "Personally, I'd like to see for myself if the legend of the Knights is true."

"Well, then I guess I better prove it to you," Ryuu said and charged him.

In a flash of movement, Maltanore met him halfway and double kicked Ryuu hard in the chest. Ryuu was launched off his feet back to the ground, where he slid across the forest floor. Clutching his chest, he looked up in time to see Maltanore flipping back to land onto his feet and slip into a low stance.

What the hell did I just get myself into? Ryuu asked himself as he curled up and leapt to his feet.

Charging each other, the two met as Ryuu tried to kick his opponent in the knee. Maltanore blocked this move with a kick, leapt up, and nailed Ryuu in the head with a kick of his own. Then he kicked Ryuu in the gut. Moaning softly, Ryuu ducked under a spin kick and, standing straight, threw a kick to Maltanore's head. Ducking under it, Maltanore swept his leg out from under Ryuu, sending him spinning face-first into the dirt.

As he started to get up, Maltanore seized him and threw him back through the air. Landing low in a stance on a boulder, Ryuu blocked a couple kicks as Maltanore leapt after him.

After ducking under a crescent kick, Maltanore blocked a second with the same leg. Then he seized Ryuu by the throat.

Thrusting his palm into Maltanore's elbow, Ryuu forced him to one knee. Then, rolling his shoulder, Maltanore stepped back and forced Ryuu down, locking Ryuu's elbow back over his shoulder.

Ryuu tried to strike out but his fist was blocked and then doubled up as Maltanore drove his forearm into his side and flipped Ryuu off his feet. Going with it, Ryuu landed on his feet and, dropping down, tried to sweep Maltanore's feet out from under him.

Standing straight, he kicked out at Maltanore, who forced the kick down, sending Ryuu flipping forward. Halfway through, he grabbed Maltanore by the ears and threw him from the boulder. Landing on his feet, he was in time to see Maltanore roll onto his back. Then, curling up, Maltanore thrust forward, landing on one knee, his leg stretched before him.

Turning to face Ryuu, he charged as Ryuu leapt over him. After blocking several more kicks, Maltanore grabbed Ryuu's arm and kicked him in his side, forcing Ryuu back before leaping at him with a hard kick. The blow launched Ryuu off his feet, and as he landed, he slammed into a thick tree trunk.

As he pushed himself to one knee, Maltanore charged him on all fours. Leaping up, Ryuu spun like a top and landed on a thick branch twenty feet up.

"Where the hell did that come from?" he asked, dazed at what he had just done. Then he spun around as he heard Maltanore land on the branch behind him.

"Before I bring this pointless but amusing exercise to an end with your death," the Anubis called, "I have a question that needs answering."

He threw a kick to Ryuu's leg, but Ryuu stepped back and it missed him.

"Oh, yeah? What's that?" Ryuu said. He stepped forward again and threw a punch.

Maltanore blocked and deflected it with both hands then backhanded Ryuu across the face. As he moved to strike again with his elbow, Ryuu blocked it, and Maltanore flicked his wrist, forcing Ryuu's strike down before backhanding him again in the head. Twisting more toward Ryuu, he nailed him with a punch to his side, sending him spinning from the branch.

As he fell, he reached out and grabbed the branch at Maltanore's feet, and as he started to pull himself up, Maltanore again seized him by the throat.

"Well?" Maltanore said. "Ready for my question?"

Before Ryuu could reply, he said, "Here it is: Why, oh why, do pests like you fight the inevitable? Why don't you just be good little insects and DIE!"

He followed up the last part with a palm strike to Ryuu's chest.

The blow sent Ryuu tumbling through the air. Hitting the ground with a roll, he stopped hard as his back scraped against a tree. Groaning, Ryuu climbed to his hands and knees.

Maltanore dropped from the branch and landed on one knee.

"Well, ANSWER ME!" he shouted as he stalked forward.

"Because . . . this . . . is . . . our . . . HOME!" Ryuu shouted. The very mention of home strengthened his resolve, and he climbed back to his feet.

Again, Maltanore charged him, and flipping like an acrobat, Ryuu sailed over him to land behind him. After blocking a kick with his knee, he kicked out at Maltanore's other knee, then bringing the same leg high, brought his heel down on his head. In rapid succession, his leg still in the air, he kicked Maltanore several times in the chest and head before Maltanore caught a sidekick.

Flipping forward as his leg was brought up he broke free before jumping up, spinning back to face him, throwing a kick which Maltanore ducked under. Landing back on his feet, Ryuu was swept off his feet by one of Maltanore's clawed hands. Landing hard on his back, he was barely able to grab Maltanore's clawed foot as he brought it down on his armored chest.

Growing with the effort, Ryuu twisted it, sending Maltanore spinning to the ground beside him. As he started to get up, he was kicked in the face, launching him back. After spinning to his feet, he was grabbed from behind and hurled against a tree.

As he started to climb to his feet, again Maltanore grabbed his shoulder and drove his fist into his gut repeatedly before punching him twice on both sides of his head. after being hit hard again in the chest, Ryuu soared back against a tree before leaping to his feet in a stance. With a roar, Maltanore leapt at him, and Ryuu brought his leg up and kicked him in his side sending him to the ground away from him.

Ryuu leapt forward, and after pushing off from a tree, he nailed Maltanore across the face with a kick. Then he fell back onto his hands to avoid a blow before springing back to his feet. From there, he kicked the Anubis in the knee, then in the head. He followed up by spinning on his own head, nailing Maltanore across the face with a kick.

Disoriented by the blows, Maltanore fell back. With a cry, Ryuu spun himself sideways through the air and brought his leg down hard across his opponent's back.

As Maltanore climbed to his feet, he rushed forward, seized Ryuu by the throat, and threw him hard against a tree.

"WARNING! WARNING!" an alarm called out in Ryuu's ear. "Further physical impacts will lead to armor retraction!"

"Good to know," he moaned. When he looked up, his eyes went wide as Maltanore ripped a tree from the ground.

"I'VE HAD ENOUGH OF THIS!" Maltanore shouted. He held the uprooted tree in both arms and swung it at Ryuu.

To dodge the swing, Ryuu leapt up into the air. But one of the roots still caught him in his midsection and sent him careening into the underbrush where he met a hard landing.

"Armor Retraction Commencing! ETA Until Operational Use Fifteen Minutes."

"A lot can happen in fifteen minutes!" Ryuu growled as a sound of metal on metal met his ears.

Some of the armor retracted off his opposite hand, moving up his arm and across his shoulder. Next, more of the armor began to retract up his legs and across his chest. As this happened, the horns on his helmet retracted into the head. Then, from the base of his throat, the helmet withdrew up and over his head. Once it reached the base of his skull, the parts over his ears slid in before it merged with the rest of the armor, which retracted across and up his chest and down his arm.

As the last of the armor melded into his bracelet, Ryuu climbed to his feet, clutching his chest. Moaning, he moved as quietly as he could through the underbrush.

At that sound of a heavy crash, he looked in the direction of Maltanore. Then he dropped flat on his chest, so that he was covered by a bush. As he inched forward, he heard the sound of a smaller thud nearby. It was followed by loud sniffs.

"I know you're here," he heard Maltanore say. "I may not see you ... but I can smell you. And my sense of smell is almost as good as a Dragon's."

Ryuu's eyes darted left and right and then focused on a flower. Holding his breath slowly, he reached for it.

Just as his fingers closed around the head, Maltanore whipped aside the bushes he'd been hiding under. Ryuu held the crushed head of the flower in his open hand and blew it hard into his enemy's face.

As Maltanore started coughing and sneezing, Ryuu took the opportunity to drop down into a dry river bed.

"That should buy me some time," he muttered. "Last time I was anywhere near that flower, I couldn't stop sneezing all day."

Minutes later, just as he arrived in the testing ground he was in the night before Maltanore dropped right in front of him, and Ryuu managed to block his punch. He did not, however, manage to avoid the powerful kick to his side. Spinning through the air, he came to a skidding, rolling stop.

Moaning as he clutched his side, Ryuu pushed himself up to watch Maltanore advance on him. His enemy was laughing.

"Well, this is certainly the icing on the cake, as humans say. Out of all the people in the known galaxies, the Legendary Armors chose a child."

"Hey, I'm still trying to figure it out myself," Ryuu countered. "Maybe it's the fact that my name means Dragon."

Hissing in pain, he pulled himself back and said, "So what happens now? You going to just kill me or make me beg, because I doubt you're going to get a better chance for bragging rights than killing a Dragon Knight!"

Maltanore started to take a step forward but froze.

Slowly his eye traveled down to the wire at his ankle level. Ryuu's eyes widened his horror as his eyes followed the wire. To the spiked log ready to swing down to impale its victim.

Chuckling Maltanore turned back to a wide eyed Ryuu. Crossing his legs, he stepped to the side and walked around Ryuu giving the trip wire a wide birth.

Until he stopped at Ryuu's side and grinned wickedly down at him. "Did you really think I would fall for the oldest trick in the book?" he leered, and with a small ringing sound and he drew a rod from the small of his back. Which expanded outward with a pair of wicked looking axe blades on either end.

For a second Ryuu just stared at him wide eyed in fear. "No," he finally said, a grin forming.

Before Maltanore could do more than blink at him. Twisting Ryuu slammed his hand down on the wire just behind him. And the blaster in a tree across from Maltanore fired the shot knocking him to the ground.

As he turned back Ryuu's armor started to expand up his arm.

"Oh, so now you work?" Ryuu muttered as the armor extended across his chest and his other arm.

At a roar Ryuu whipped around. To see Maltanore soar through the air arms outstretched to grab him. Reacting he leapt into a tree and out of sight.

Leaping after him, Maltanore crashed onto the same branch. Finding Ryuu no longer there. "NO MORE TRICKS! THIS

ENDS NOW!" he roared, spinning on the spot as he searched for Ryuu. "WHERE ARE YOU?"

In response, Ryuu, now fully armored, ran down the trunk of the tree. A rod at his hip shot into his hands.

"HERE, DOGGY, DOGGY!" Ryuu shouted. He leapt from the tree at Maltanore, who turned to face him, both slashing out at each other.

With a r Ryuu landed on the ground below Maltanore and stopped on one knee. Behind him, he heard a soft thump, followed by a heavier thump. When Ryuu turned around, he saw Maltanore's body lying on the ground, the head of the Anubis on the mossy ground beside him.

Slowly, his eyes moved down to look at the rod in his hand. The katana blade that extended from the rod was made of an almost transparent light. He watched as the blade slowly retracted back into the rod. When the blade disappeared entirely, he let it go, and the rod reattached itself to his hip.

"Boy, am I glad that's over. He was really kicking my butt," Ryuu muttered. Breathing hard, he sagged down, hands on his thighs.

Back in the village, Allison was fighting with the Dark Elf. As he landed on the ground, he heard the Dark Elf say, "You know, I find myself disappointed. If this is the best the Knights of old could do, they must have won their battles by intimidation alone."

"Well, at least I'm not a betrayer of my own people!" Allison snapped. She climbed to her feet and charged at her opponent.

With an amused look on her face, the Dark Elf stepped to the side, avoiding Allison's kick. Then, she snatched Allison out of mid-air and threw her against a hover car that was turned on its side. The car crumpled under the impact, and the Dark Elf drew her hand through the air, producing a dark, elegant sword in a flash of light.

"Bold words for a little girl about to die," she said. She advanced toward Allison, sword in hand.

❉

Suddenly, Ryuu appeared out of nowhere sailing through the air and nailed the Dark Elf with a hard flying sidekick. It launched the Elf off her feet, and she rolled across the ground

"You forgot one thing about Knights," he snapped. "We always come in packs!"

"You okay?" he asked as Allison stumbled toward him.

"I had her right where I wanted her," she muttered, clutching her shoulder.

"I don't doubt it," Ryuu replied.

The Elf climbed to her feet. "You! Where's Maltanore?"

"Oh, you mean this guy?" Ryuu lifted the object in his hand, and the Elf recoiled when she saw it was Maltanore's disembodied head.

"Guess he didn't have the head for this job," he said. Then he tossed the head at her feet.

The Elf looked from the head of the Anubis to Ryuu. Then her gaze wandered as a crowd of people, including Eric, gathered behind them.

"Might I have the pleasure of your name? So I know a walking dead man," she said, placing one hand behind her.

Ryuu was silent for a moment, not sure of what to say. Then, standing straight, he declared, "Just call me Robin Hood."

As the Elf started to laugh, Allison leaned closer to Ryuu.

She whispered, "Robin Hood? Are you kidding me?"

Glancing at his friend, he muttered, "What? That's been my nickname from you guys for years."

"Yeah, a nickname, not an alias!"

The Elf snickered. Then she said, "So, young man, you wish to

100

remake a legend. If that's the case, I personally prefer heroes with a sense of tragedy in their past."

Seconds later, she thrust her hand out from behind her back. Resting in the middle of her palm was a fiery ball of energy, which she launched from her hand. Eyes growing wide, Ryuu watched in slow motion as the ball soared through the air and collided into Eric, who raised his arms as if to shield himself. When it exploded, the shock sent both Ryuu and Allison flying. Ryuu landed hard. As he rolled across the ground, he looked back to the smoke-filled crater. There was no way to tell if Erik had survived.

Glancing down at Allison, he saw her freeze in horror. Baring his teeth, Ryuu turned to pursue the Dark Elf, who was now running toward the transport.

"This thing have any long-range weapons?" he yelled into his helmet mask. As he glanced at his holo armor readout, he saw that the icons of his lower arms, hips, and the small of his back started to flash.

"Well, this will have to do," he said, reaching behind him.

From the small of his back, he pulled a rod with a slight angled indentation on either side of the grip. As he brought it forward, limbs of a bow shot out from each end, with a laser string shooting from the top to the bottom. Skidding to a stop, he reached over his shoulder for an arrow but felt nothing.

"Great, now what am I to do with this? Hit her with it?" he shouted as he flicked the string.

At once, what looked like an arrow made of light appeared and shot from the bow. It launched through the air and caused an overturned hover car to jump into the sky and fall back to the ground, making a fiery wreck.

"Okay, that'll work!" he said. Then he drew back the string, turned, and aimed at the back of the retreating Elf.

As he did, a movement in the sky caught his eye. He watched frozen as Aiolos and Bryan weaved through the air, dodging laser fire from the last fighter. Glancing back down, he saw that the Elf was almost back at the transport.

After a couple seconds of shifting his aim, he gave a cry and fired. He watched as the arrow streaked through the air and slammed onto one of the wings of the fighter, which tumbled, spinning from the air, and crashed into the ground between the transport and the Elf.

"OH, YEAH! NOW THAT WAS A HELL OF A SHOT!" Ryuu yelled. He jumped into the air, whooping and brandishing the bow. "YES!"

Turning around he let loose a giant sigh of relief, Allison raced toward Erik, who was now visible through the smoke that continued to rise in front of some of the villagers. The ground before them looked like it had been scooped away. Erik's arms were still crossed in front of his face, and the crystal on his bracelet was pulsing to the same rhythm as a flashing shield, which had formed in front of him. Slowly he lowered his arms, and the shield vanished just as Allison reached him, knocking him to the ground in a ferocious hug.

A shout from Bryan caught Ryuu's attention, and when he turned he saw Bryan and Aiolos on the ground standing over the Dark Elf.

"Don't even think about it!" Bryan snapped as the Dark Elf started to get up.

Ryuu moved toward them, and Allison and Erik quickly followed.

As Ryuu reached them, his bow retracted, and he replaced it at the small of his back. He faced the Dark Elf and said, "Now what was that you were saying about us being pests? Got to be careful, because they have a habit of multiplying."

Then a new voice came from behind him. "And I thought I taught you better than to gloat over a wounded enemy." It was Jun.

Ryuu whipped around to face his father. "Hey, after what they did, we deserve a little glo—" He caught himself halfway and stopped. "I have no idea what you're talking about," he quickly said, trying to cover up.

"Son, you were never a good liar to me or your mother. We know your tell too good, no matter how slight."

Ryuu was silent for a moment before his shoulders slumped. "Sorry, Dad."

"Too much sugar, eh?" his father said, crossing his arms.

Ryuu made sure enough blasters were on the Dark Elf. Then he gave his father his full attention. Behind his helmet mask, Ryuu gave a weak smile.

"Eh, I can explain . . . but for right now . . . eh, how do you get this armor off? I doubt it's like we can say *deactivate*."

Before he could continue, a voice in his ear interrupted his train of thought. "Armor Retraction Commencing."

At once, with the sound of metal on metal, the armor retracted into itself.

Raising his hand, Ryuu watched as the last of the armor melded into the bracelet. Staring in amazement and shock, he shifted his eyes up to his friends, who were staring back at him. One by one, they deactivated their armor. Then they gathered around Ryuu's family, who were standing at the front of a group of villagers.

Looking at his father, Ryuu opened his mouth to speak, but his father raised his hand.

Jun said, "I was going to be angry, but that was before the next generation of Dragon Knights stood before us." Then he slowly knelt before them.

Stepping back in surprise, Ryuu looked at his mother. She beamed at him before she, too, knelt before them. The friends exchanged puzzled glances as row by row the villagers knelt before them. At the very back was Dulglad and his father, and after a few seconds, they, too, knelt.

CHAPTER 11
LIVE FOR FREEDOM . . . DIE FOR FREEDOM

"OKAY, THIS IS a little awkward," Aiolos muttered.

Before Ryuu could reply, he was knocked off his feet as the ground beneath him shook.

"WHAT THE—" he started to shout. He stopped when he saw the trails of hundreds of missiles and the clouds of their explosions. "Armageddon Missiles," he muttered in fear, as great cracks in the earth opened up around him.

"EVERYONE IN THE TRANSPORT, NOW!" his father screamed, pointing at the remaining ship on the ground.

Almost immediately, the villagers started running for the ship. Ryuu and the others regained their feet and followed.

"There must be other ships in orbit!" Allison yelled. "They must have some idea what happened down here, or else they wouldn't be doing this!"

"Well, this is typical of the Black Dragon's forces!" Ryuu replied, running full out for the boarding ramp. "Blow up a whole planet just because they believe an enemy to be on it!"

Less than ten feet from the ship, Ryuu came to a skidding stop as he heard a scream come from behind him. He turned and saw the ground beneath the Elf crumble and vanish under her feet, and she fell with another piercing scream.

Before he had time to think about it, he leapt forward toward the edge of the chasm. Landing flat on the ground, he thrust a hand down and caught her by the wrist.

"I've got you!" he shouted as she stared at him in amazement.

Before she could say anything, a crumbling sound met their ears. Looking under him, he saw the ledge he was on begin to fall away.

"You can let go, human . . . I'd understand," she said in a hollow voice.

Looking back at her, he desperately shouted, "Somebody! Help me!"

When no one came, she gave him a small smile and closed her eyes. At once, her features underwent a transformation. The ridge on her head vanished, and her skin turned white and fair. When she opened her eyes, Ryuu saw that they were now a deep violet.

"Prove him wrong, young knight," she muttered. Then she released her grip on him and slipped from his grasp.

"NO!" he bellowed, wide-eyed with horror as she fell into the abyss.

For a few seconds, he remained there, too stunned to move. The sound of the ledge beginning to fall snapped him back to reality as he tipped forward. Suddenly, a pair of strong hands grabbed him by his shirt and, with a mighty tug, dragged him to safety.

He landed on his side and turned to look into his rescuer's eyes.

"Alec-Ryuu, don't you ever freeze up like that again!" his father shouted, giving him a rough shake by the upper arms. "You're too important to lose!"

Then Jun nodded toward the transport ship. "I can't explain now, but you, your friends, your mother, and the rest of the village must take that ship."

"But Dad, what about you," Ryuu said.

Jun grasped Ryuu's arm. "I'll out-run any other ship they have in orbit in one of the escape transports," he finished. "Then I will rendezvous with you all when I can."

"You'll never make it!" Ryuu cried. He looked up just as the mountain above them seemed to split in half and magma began flowing.

"We don't have time for an argument," Jun shouted at him. "Now move!" He pushed Ryuu toward the transport before turning.

"No, Dad! I won't let you go! It's suicide!" Ryuu grabbed Jun by the shoulder.

At that, Jun lowered his head. "I'm sorry," he muttered, and before Ryuu could do or say anything, his father whirled around, raised a fist, and Ryuu's world went black.

After knocking out Ryuu with a single strike, Jun gently reached out and took the young man in his arms before he could fall to the ground.

"Jun, what the hell is the matter with you?" Chikako demanded, running up with another villager.

He looked at her with tears in his eyes. Then he said, "Our boy and his friends have been chosen to fulfill a great destiny! They're Dragon Knights now, and they must be protected at all costs. It could mean our survival! And the survival of all free people! This was the only way I could get Ryuu to go."

For a few seconds, they looked at each other. Then tears began to stream down Chikako's cheeks.

"You're right," she said quietly. Then she reached out, took Ryuu from her husband, and handed him to the villager.

"Please carry my son to the transport," she said.

Jun took her hand. "Now I'm going to be the decoy. Once they're after me, you get the hell out!" he said.

Slowly Chikako nodded. She started to walk toward the transport. Then she ran back and flung herself into his arms.

Jun kissed his wife gently and said, "Until we meet again, my love."

This time, when they parted, she ran all the way to the transport. Jun watched as she disappeared inside as the ramp was raised.

As the world came apart around him, Jun stood still for a few seconds. Then he darted around the chasms and made his way to the forest. At the edge, he stopped before a tree and pressed hard onto a knot. The tree split open, revealing an elevator. He jumped in, and it immediately lowered below ground, stopping at the entrance to a large hangar.

Inside the hangar, a line of ships awaited on landing skids. Most were as large as a bus, with a point pod section in the front and a smooth shaft that extended in the back, where a set of stubby wings with engines at the tips reached out from all four sides. With his heart racing, Jun ran up the ramp of the nearest ship.

Once inside, he hit a holo button on the side. Immediately the ramp retracted and the hatch closed, sealing itself. Not stopping, Jun raced to the front and into the cockpit, which was a plain, two-seated area with the controls in front and above the seats. Jumping into pilot's seat Jun flipped switches and pressed holo buttons, and the ship came to life. The viewing screens in front and to the sides of the seats flicked on, as well as a holographic globe, which floated between the two seats and displayed various sensor readouts.

At a crashing sound, he looked out the screen to his right and saw the far wall break open. Lave poured into the hangar, melting the ships as it went. Grabbing the throttle, he threw it all the way back, and the ship rocketed forward. The movement threw him back against his seat, and the auto straps shot out and secured him to the chair. Yoke in his hands, he flew at a breakneck speed through the caverns, which was falling apart around him.

Coming around a sharp turn to the opening, he saw lava and

rocks pouring back into the cave and fire spurting out around the edges. He gritted his teeth and opened the throttle all the way. He gave a sharp cry as the ship shot forward and through the flames, rocketing into the sky.

When he glanced out at the nearest view screen, his eyes widened at the horrendous sight before him. The forest that had covered the area surrounding the village and mountains where the school had been was now gone. It looked like a giant had come through and ripped and burned the trees from the land that they had been a part of.

Climbing higher and higher into the sky, he could see just how deep and far the cracks extended, and even from inside the ship, he could hear the roar of the earth as the existing cracks grew and new ones appeared. The sound of the small eruptions as it spurted up out of the ground and the roar of the lava, which bubbled like many geysers, pulled at his heart. To him, in every sense of the phrase, it was indeed hell.

Unable to look at the sight anymore, he faced forward again as he soared through the clouds and into the stars. Closing his eyes, he wiped a tear away and sagged against the safety straps that held him to the chair.

Moments later, the shrill sound of the alarms blaring caused him to sit bolt upright and look at the sensor globe.

Seeing the ships coming after him, he banked his vessel hard to the right, activating the shields.

"Dad! Dad, do you read me?" Ryuu's voice came over the com link.

"Alec?" he said.

"Six ships in pursuit!"

Looking back at the globe, he could see the blips closing the distance between them. "I know," he muttered.

"But you can't out-run them in that bucket of bolts! Adjust

heading one, one three five, and we'll cover you," Ryuu shouted at him.

Jun was silent for a moment as he watched the ships draw ever closer. Then he turned and looked out the forward view screen again.

"Ryuu, I'm sorry. Now you and your friends must listen to me carefully. There's not much time." As he spoke, the ships started firing on him, and he maneuvered his vessel carefully.

"Fate has entrusted you and your friends with a sacred mission, Alec. The spirits of the Dragons of old have chosen you and your friends to be the next generation of Dragon Knights, the greatest of responsibilities, Ryuu. You all must surrender to your shared destiny wherever it may lead you."

He took a deep breath and continued. "As for me, I have one last fatherly duty to perform for you my son." He was jolted in his seat as the ship rocked from a direct hit and the alarms sounded.

"DAD!"

Pressing buttons to seal off the breaches, he turned back to check his shield gauges and saw they were failing.

"Now I give my final instructions to you as your father and your sensei. You must find the Sherwood, the other parts of you, your birth mother, and the next Gold Dragon. Find them and this war will end."

A new blip appeared on the sensor readout as one of the ships fired a missile.

"Live for freedom . . . die for freedom," he muttered. Then he closed his eyes and the vessel exploded.

CHAPTER 12
ROBIN HOOD

ON THE TRANSPORT, Ryuu, his friends, and his mother stared frozen in horror at the com as nothing but static came through. Ryuu lowered his head and sobbed. On his wrist, the crystal on his bracelet pulsed as his tears struck it.

When he finally raised his head and looked outside the ship, he saw that the cracks on their planet were growing larger and deeper, spreading across the surface with a deep-red glow. Moments later, the planet exploded, sending a shockwave of debris straight at the transport. Getting closer and closer, it raced at the little ship like a giant wave that's set to smash a small shell into pieces.

The second before the shockwave reached the ship, Ryuu heard the engines give a small clap like thunder and a throbbing pulse. Then it jumped into hyperspace, to safety.

✿

Hours later, they were still in hyperspace. Ryuu stood alone in a corridor of the ship, leaning against the force field portal, his hands on either side of his head as grief continued to flood through him. With his tears still falling, he was overwhelmed with images and memories of his father: his recent birthday, his training, their home-work sessions, the family's game nights, and love. Always love.

Behind him, he heard his friends and mother come into the cor-ridor. For a moment, they stood in silence. Then his mother walked forward until they were side by side.

His mother rubbed a comforting hand along his shoulder and he closed his eyes for a moment. When he opened them again, he looked out at the blurred stars that were flashing by. On his wrist, the crystal on his bracelet pulsed a few times.

Finally, his mother spoke. "As long as a shred of evil exists in the uni-verse, there will always be a fight for freedom. That's what your father believed." She sniffed loudly. "And the fact is that he and your birth mother fought together in the Resistance against The Black Dragon."

She lowered her gaze, and he looked at her in surprise.

"He never said, anything," Ryuu muttered.

"Before we settled down, the fighters used to say that if the armors hadn't been seized by the Black Dragon, Jun would have been a Dragon Knight. He never would have admitted it, but it was his dream," his mother continued. Ryuu glanced at his bracelet, which pulsed again.

She looked out at the sky and said, "Good-bye, my love. May clear stars guide you home." Then she wiped some tears from her face.

"What did he mean?" Ryuu asked. "When he said, 'find . . . the other parts of you,' what did he mean?"

She was still for a moment. Then she turned to face him, and he could see that she was crying again.

"When your birth mother came to us, you weren't the only one she gave birth to. You have a brother and sister," she said. "You were all born on the same day."

Ryuu and his friends all stared at her. His jaw dropped, his eyes widened, and his tears stopped. "Wha . . . I have a brother . . . and a sister . . ."

He paused and tried to absorb what he had heard. "Why didn't you tell me?" he demanded.

"Your birth mother made us promise not to tell you until you were ready. We were going to tell you today when we realized . . . then all this." She waved her hands about.

"I'll give you some time alone," she said quietly. Then she turned and left.

Ryuu's friends gathered around him.

"Well, this has been a hell of a day," Allison said.

For a couple moments, the group stood there in silence before Bryan broke it.

"You know, I think I understand how you must feel, Ryuu—"

"That's not my name anymore," Ryuu said flatly.

He looked at his friends, who flinched.

"Alec-Ryuu Jun Yamamoto died back on Amal. From here on out, my name is Robin Hood," Ryuu, now Robin Hood said. His voice and face were hard.

One by one, his friends looked from him to each other.

"Well, it was already a nickname, so Little John suits me just fine," Bryan, now Little John, said. He crossed his arms.

"I guess it would be appropriate for me to bear the name Tuck," Eric, now Tuck, said.

"I could settle for Willa Scarlet," Allison, now Willa, said, after glancing at her brother.

Looking around at his friends, Aiolos smiled. "I guess it's up to me to be the cool Much."

Robin smiled briefly at his friends and then turned to look out again at the stars.

For a couple seconds, Robin was still. Then he looked down at his bracelet. Raising it, he ran his fingertips over the pulsing crystal.

"We'll find them," he promised. "We'll find the Sherwood, the other knights, my brother and sister, and my birth mother. And most of all, we'll make the Black Dragon pay for what he did on this wretched day."

Dragon Knights Chronicles Book 2:

BLOOD CALLS

TIME HAD NO meaning to Robin as he sat against the hull of the cargo hold. He tried to ignore the rumbles from his stomach and the irritating scratching of his desert-dry throat.

Freya had finally gotten to sleep after shedding what seemed like a day and a night's worth of tears. He glanced down at her as she used his lap for a pillow. Then he gently patted her head, trying not to hit her with the laser manacle on his arm.

The people around them moaned from either hunger or thirst. Slowly his eyes tracked over to the water and food units. Both were bone dry now.

"You'd think with such precious cargo they'd take better care of us . . ." His voice came out in a rough croak.

His thoughts were interrupted by the sounds of a scuffle. Looking over, he saw Hannah struggling with a man over a few morsels of food that the man had managed to horde. When it started to get violent, Robin used what little strength he had left to move Freya's head from his lap and climb to his feet.

He shuffled over to the pair and pulled them apart. "That's enough!" he barked, and several people turned and stared.

"All I wanted was a little bit of food for my child," Hannah explained. Robin kept one hand on her shoulder and the other on the man's chest.

"And I warned her that if she touched my stash again, meat would be back on the menu for her child!" the man snapped. He continued to shield the meager food with his hands.

At once Robin turned on him. "They've already taken our freedom . . . should we let them take our humanity too? Because if we don't stick together, it will take them easy less time to break us or wipe us out."

For a few seconds, the man held his gaze. Then the man slowly lowered his eyes and opened his hands, revealing a chunk of stale bread no bigger than a fist.

Slowly, Robin extended his own hand and said, "What if it was your child?"

The man scowled. "If it was my child, I make sure it learned that the best way to survive is to look out for yourself." He sat back down.

Robin sighed and shook his head. Then he returned his focus to the woman, who gave a sob and fell to her knees. Dropping down next to her, he laid a comforting hand on her shoulder.

When she finally looked at him, he said, "Come on; we still have some food." He helped her up and the two went for her daughter.

A short while later, Robin and Freya watched as the mother eagerly fed the young toddler.

"If we weren't slaves, I'd suggest you go into politics," Freya said, and Robin looked at her. "Damn near had me convinced, and I wasn't the only one."

After looking at her for a second, he cocked a half grin. "It'd drive me crazy. Probably end up shooting myself my first term," he said, and she laughed.

Suddenly the laser cord on Robin's manacle turned on, and the next thing he knew, he was being dragged across the floor by his arm. He came to a sudden stop next to Takmet, and the band of lasers shackled the pair close to each other.

"This again," he moaned. When he sat up and looked around, he realized that half the people were also sprawled across the floor after being dragged across it. "I guess we've arrived."

He had no sooner said the words when the cargo doors opened. Behind them stood three Sentinels.

"On your feet, all of you!" they barked in mechanical voices. They slid their laser whips out from under their forearms, into their hands, and started cracking them.

Robin stole a glance over at Freya, who was chained with the toddler's mother. The older woman was trying to keep close to her daughter, who was chained to a middle-aged man.

"We said on your feet!"

The sharp sting of the whip brought Robin back. He bit back the pain, cringed slightly, and climbed to his feet.

"Now move!" the Sentinel barked, and they were all marched out of the ship to the sounds of roaring applause.

CPSIA information can be obtained
at www.ICGtesting.com
Printed in the USA
LVOW13s1514051017
551320LV00012B/937/P